The New BLACK MASK

The New BLACK MASK

Number 7

EDITED BY

MATTHEW J. BRUCCOLI & RICHARD LAYMAN

A HARVEST/HBJ BOOK

HARCOURT BRACE JOVANOVICH, PUBLISHERS

SAN DIEGO   NEW YORK   LONDON

Editorial correspondence should be directed to the editors at Bruccoli Clark Publishers, Inc., 2006 Sumter Street, Columbia, SC 29201.

ISSN 0884-8963
ISBN 0-15-665486-5

Designed by G. B. D. Smith

Printed in the United States of America

First Harvest/HBJ edition 1986

A B C D E F G H I J

HBJ

Contents

Ed McBain: An Interview

Nineteen eighty-six is a year of celebration for Ed McBain. It is the thirtieth anniversary of the first 87th Precinct novel, the year in which the thirty-ninth novel in the series will be published, and at the Mystery Writers of America (MWA) awards dinner, he will be given the highest honor the MWA bestows—Grand Master—in recognition of a distinguished body of work. In 1959, Anthony Boucher observed in his introduction to an omnibus of the first three 87th Precinct novels that "at exactly the right historical moment [McBain] managed to write, with more striking effect than anyone before him, what readers were hungering for and whetted their appetites." Since that time, Mr. McBain has shown a remarkable ability to keep on satisfying his audience, adapting his material to the times and attracting a new generation of readers as appreciative as those Boucher described a quarter century ago.

Ed McBain is the pseudonym of Evan Hunter.

NBM: During the past thirty years, you have written some forty 87th Precinct novels in which you described a fictional city and a fictional police force so rich in detail that they have prompted a book-length study of the geography of the precinct, the characterizations of the 87th Precinct detectives, and even the crime statistics of the city. Did you begin the series with the intention of creating the fictional city of Isola piece by piece?

1

McBain: No, not really. When I first proposed the idea, I said I wanted to do a story about a conglomerate detective hero. Herb Alexander at Pocket Books came to me originally. Erle Stanley Gardner was getting old, and he was the mainstay of Pocket Books. They would keep bringing out his books with new covers every couple of months and they would just sell like crazy, but he was getting old and Pocket Books was looking for a replacement, to be blunt about it, and he asked me if I had any ideas for a series character. I proposed the notion of doing a conglomerate detective hero, so that all the detectives in the squad room, when put together, would make the hero. I wanted to set it in New York City, and I wanted it to be as realistic and as gritty as it possibly could be. When I started the series, the actual writing of it, after doing a lot of research in New York, I discovered that I was spending a great deal of time on the telephone with the NYPD, and I thought, this is going to be serious trouble. I had a contract for three books, and I thought, if this does indeed become a successful series and goes on from those three books, I'll be calling the cops every five minutes. So I decided to make it a mythical city. A lot of people have said that Isola is New York, but it really isn't. I mean, it is, but it isn't. It's almost impossible to fit together the pieces of the jigsaw and make it New York City. I've had a lot of fun over the years inventing historical facts for this city that doesn't exist, and naming places, and going into the derivation of the names, and all that.

NBM: Has your concept of the city changed over the past thirty years?

McBain: Maybe not mine, but Carella's certainly has. In all of the new books he comments on the graffiti and the lack of services and the difficulty of getting anything done on time. He's gotten a bit crankier over the years and a bit less patient with bureacuracy, I think.

NBM: Is that because he has to live in the city and you get to live in Florida?

McBain: I never really lived in the city except as a boy, you know. I lived in Manhattan until I was twelve years old and then we moved up to the Bronx. And we were poor. After I was married we lived in the Bronx again, and then later we moved out to Long Island. But I never lived in the city with the economic means to enjoy it. It seems to me that New York is a city of very poor people and very rich people, and the ones in between have a real struggle trying to make a good life for themselves.

NBM: One of the marks of a long mystery series is that after a while the characters become stale and the plots seem contrived, as the author struggles to avoid repetition. How have you been able to avoid these problems in the 87th Precinct series? Is there something inherent in the police procedural form that produces fresh material in novel after novel?

McBain: No. I think the strength of the series is the characters in it. The mysteries are pretty good, I hope. But I think the characters are what make the series

3

work and what the readers out there are really most interested in. As an example, in *Poison,* and in the excerpt you're running from *Poison,* Hal Willis is at center stage. He has been sort of a supporting player up to now. We know very little about his past. It has only been sketched in: he's a judo expert, and he's short. These are the tics that identify him when he comes on stage. Well, in *Poison* he has *center* stage. Carella is his sidekick, in effect. What I try to do to keep the series fresh for me is come up with good ideas for a mystery that will keep the reader guessing and entertained. That's my first job; that's my contract with the reader. But I also try to find something fresh and new about the characters each time, so that I can add to their characterizations in each book. If you come to the series fresh, you'll meet someone you haven't met before, but if you've been with the series for the past thirty years, you'll find out something new about the characters in each of the books. That's what keeps it fresh for me. I must tell you I don't consciously sit down and say, "How am I going to make this one fresh this time?" I never feel that the series is getting stale, so I don't have to worry about making it fresh.

NBM: Haven't you been quoted as saying that Ed McBain is an entertainer and Evan Hunter is a more serious writer?

McBain: No, I don't think I said exactly that. Mickey Spillane said, "I'm just an entertainer. I'm not a writer; I'm an entertainer." I've always wondered why he said that. No, I think it's also my job in an Evan Hunter novel to keep the reader entertained. A person can be doing any number of other things besides reading a book. I myself have very little patience with a book when I'm twenty pages into it and the writer is examining his own navel. I don't feel that's what writing should be all about. If I can write fiction that illuminates something for a reader out there, the only way I'm going to be able to throw any illumination on any particular aspect of life is to keep the reader reading. And that means keeping him entertained.

NBM: Are you any more or less likely to be illuminating as Ed McBain?

McBain: I don't think so. I feel that for many, many years in this country the mystery novel was looked down upon. I guess it started when Edmund Wilson wrote "Who Cares Who Killed Roger Ackroyd?" Well, *I* do. I feel when I'm writing a mystery that I'm writing about life and death, and I can't think of anything more important than that to write about. So I don't just toss off these mysteries, and I don't feel that the reader is reading them *only* to have a puzzle presented to him and *only* to be entertained. I think along the way he learns a lot about crime and punishment in a big city, and that to me is important.

NBM: To what extent are you inspired to write a novel by some actual crime or some actual criminal?

McBain: Not at all. I figure that if an actual crime is important enough, then it will have gotten all the press and media coverage that it warrants, and for me to go back to it and do it all over again is just a waste of the reader's time and my time. So I never base any

5

of my mysteries on actual crimes. I will occasionally *refer* to something that happened. As an example, there were some guys who drove into a city street in New York and began digging up the cobblestones on the street and loading them into a truck. Everybody just watched them; they thought they were workers for the city who were repairing the street, or that they were taking the cobblestones away so they could pave the street next week, or whatever. That's the way things happen in New York. But they were *thieves!* They stole a whole city street. They loaded the cobblestones into the truck and drove off with them. I used that in one of the novels. I will sometimes use funny little incidents that actually occur in New York, that you read about all the time. I'll use those in the books to give a flavor, to show what can happen in a big city. But never, never do I base any of my books on actual crimes.

NBM: Are you still researching after thirty years?

McBain: By accident, more or less. I have a small reputation as a mystery writer, and especially as a writer of police novels. I do a lot of television work. When producers out there think of someone who would be good to do a pilot about cops, they'll think of me, and they'll ask me to work on it. So, over the past several years the research continues, and not only in New York City. I did a half-hour pilot—none of these go on, you understand, because in television it's a long, long trip from the cup to the lip, believe me—but I did a pilot on the 911 emergency cops in New York, so I had to spend a couple of weeks with them. I did a pilot on the cops in Houston, so I had to spend time with the cops

6

in Houston. I did a pilot on the New Orleans police and spent time with them. You know, cops all over the country are pretty much the same. Their routine doesn't vary. They may be more or less equipped to deal with crime than cops in a big, big city like New York or Chicago, but for the most part they are all cut from the same cloth. I learn a lot about policemen by working on these things and it all filters into the 87th Precinct.

NBM: I think many people may have been surprised to learn recently, through a series in *Armchair Detective*, that Elmore Leonard employs a researcher to prepare reports about the places and subjects he uses in his novels.

McBain: I don't normally do that. I do it with some of the Evan Hunter novels. The most recent example is *Lizzie*, about Lizzie Borden. That was a monumental job of research, and I could not have done it alone. I had a researcher help me with that. With *Poison* I had a researcher help me. It's a very complicated plot, and I needed help with working out the details. I had *Poison* in mind for many, many years, and I was just too damn lazy to do the research. I had the idea of how the murder could be committed, and I was just too lazy to get down to it and say, "Okay, now let's figure out the actualites of it."

NBM: Do you aim for an ideal reader?

McBain: No. I get a lot of mail from readers, and they're all different kinds of people. So, I can't base what I write on the mail I get, because it would be too confusing. Yet I always have a reader in mind when

7

I'm writing. I mean when I tell a joke in a book, I hope that my sense of humor will click with some anonymous person who will share my sense of humor. When I'm writing, if the hackles are going up on the back of my neck, then I hope I'm writing a scene that's scary enough for a reader to be scared as well. I think what I'm looking for is a reader who shares my sensibilities and who will appreciate them. I guess that's what causes people to read books anyway. If you like Ludlum, you read Ludlum; and if you like Leonard, you read Leonard. There is something about the writer that transmits itself to the reader, who enjoys it and continues reading it. But I don't have an ideal reader in mind. Just someone who is intelligent, who appreciates a puzzle and a sense of humor, and who wants solid characterization. I guess that's the reader I aim for.

NBM: Are you affected as a writer by what you read?

McBain: I guess you're affected as a writer by everything you read, everything you see, every place you visit. I sometimes feel the IRS should allow me to deduct my whole life.

NBM: Are you a reader of mysteries?

McBain: Rarely. You know, I don't think I've read a book in the past year. It's a terrible admission for a writer to make, but at the end of the day I'm so tired of dealing with words and juggling words and shuffling words and moving them around to get what I want, that I don't want to look at any more words. So I'll watch television for an hour or so and then I'll go to sleep.

NBM: Do you write every day?

McBain: Every day from nine to five. Although here in Florida I seem to get the quota done earlier for some reason. I'm usually through here at about three, which is nice. Maybe it's the incentive to get outside and enjoy the wonderful weather.

NBM: Since Pocket Books introduced the 87th Precinct novels, there have been five hardback publishers of the series: Simon and Schuster, allied with Pocket Books, of course; Delacorte; Random House; Viking; and now Arbor House. Why so many changes?

McBain: Well, I always give a publisher a fair shot, you know, but I want to see where a publisher is *going* with the series. The series has been around a long time now, and immodestly, I think it's pretty damn good. It constantly puzzles me that the 87th Precinct novels are not best-sellers. Why do they not immediately get on the best-seller list? Whom are we not reaching out there? When a publisher tells me the books are very good, and we're going to stick with it, and we're going to edge it up two thousand copies a year, I say to the publisher, "I haven't got that much time. I'll be ninety-eight years old when a book finally gets on the best-seller list." You must remember, I was with these publishers for a long, long time. I was with Simon and Schuster for God knows how long; I was with Doubleday for ten years, I think. Random House and Viking I really did not feel were getting all the way behind the series and giving it what it needed. Arbor House has done a good job to date. I just delivered the last book

9

under the contract to them. I don't know what'll happen there, we'll see. But writers change publishers because they aren't doing the job.

NBM: Do you subscribe to the notion that mystery writers are underappreciated?

McBain: Oh, absolutely. Not as underappreciated as they used to be; the evidence is there that mysteries *do* pop up on the best-seller list with a great deal of regularity. So, no publisher who's aware of marketing would ever say that mysteries are not a viable commodity. But, you see, publishing has changed so much since the early days that there is very little loyalty—going both ways, from publisher to writer or from writer to publisher. Writers come and go now. I have heard it said by agents and I've even heard it said by editors that if only publishers could publish books without having to deal with writers, they'd be very happy. I think very often that is the case. Publishing has become such a big-time business. It's all linked with television. We see so much trash on television that publishers feel the way to steal the television market is to publish trash. It's an unfortunate situation. So one constantly looks for the ideal publisher.

NBM: Having established yourself as a visual writer, and having had success as a screenwriter, have you ever been tempted to give up book publishing altogether and go into screenwriting full-time?

McBain: Not really. I have a big television production coming up on April 13 that I'm very proud of—*Dream West*, with Richard Chamberlain and a whole great, wonderful cast of actors. I think it's going to be on the screen as I wrote it, at least I've got my fingers crossed. This was a good project from the very beginning. The people I was working with were all professionals, and the experience was so enjoyable that, yes, it can get very tempting. You think, why am I writing books when I can hit eighty million people in one night? And the money, of course, is better in screenwriting, so it's very tempting to say the hell with book writing. But I love writing books, and many television projects or motion-picture projects are not as agreeable as this one was. You get locked into some project where a lot of other people are involved, and it's not just you sitting at your machine. There are all these other people, and sometimes it becomes unpleasant. So, though I've been tempted, I've never decided to give up book writing entirely and go strictly for television or movies.

NBM: Did you have anything to do with *Hill Street Blues*? Did they come to you when they were developing the series?

McBain: No, they did not come to me. It continues to amaze me that anyone developing a police series, a series with a conglomerate hero in a mythical city, had never heard of the 87th Precinct. My only consolation is that *Hill Street Blues* will be off the air one day, and I'll still be here writing my novels.

Honesty

ED McBAIN

The following is an excerpt from Poison, *Ed Mc-Bain's forthcoming 87th Precinct novel.*

BY EIGHT O'CLOCK that night, Willis had talked to all three men on the short list of "friends" Marilyn Hollis had less than graciously provided, and he figured it was time he paid the lady herself another visit.

He did not call first.

Unannounced and uninvited, he drove to 1211 Harborside Lane, and parked his car at the curb adjacent to the small park across the street from her building. It was still bitterly cold. March had come in like a lion and was going out like a lion, so much for the *Farmer's Almanac* disciples. The wind tossing his hair, his face raw after only a short walk from his car across the street, he rang the front doorbell and waited.

Her voice over the speaker said, "Mickey?"

"No," he said, "it's Detective Willis."

There was a long silence.

"What do you want?" she said.

"Few questions I'd like to ask you. If you have a minute."

"I'm sorry, I can't talk to you just now," she said. "I'm expecting someone."

"When can I come back?" he asked.

"How about never?" she said, and he could swear she was smiling.

"How about later tonight?" he said.

"No, I'm sorry."

"Miss Hollis, this is a homicide..."

"I'm sorry," she said again.

There was a click. And then silence.

He pressed the doorbell button again.

"Listen," she said over the speaker, "I'm truly sorry, but..."

"Miss Hollis," he said, "do I have to get a warrant just to *talk* to you?"

Silence.

Then: "All right, come in."

13

The buzzer sounded. He grabbed for the doorknob and let himself into the entrance foyer. Another buzzer sounded, unlocking the inner door. He opened the door and stepped tentatively into the paneled living room. A fire was going in the fireplace across the room. Incense was burning. Not a sign of her anywhere.

He closed the door behind him.

"Miss Hollis?" he called.

"I'm upstairs. Take off your coat, sit down. I'm on the phone."

He hung his coat on a rack just inside the door, and then sat close to the door in a chair upholstered in red crushed velvet. Mickey, he thought. Mickey who? He waited. He could hear nothing from the upstairs levels of the house. The fire crackled and spit. He waited. Still no sounds from upstairs.

"Miss Hollis?" he called again.

"Be with you in a minute!" she called back.

He'd been waiting for at least ten minutes when finally she came down the walnut-banistered staircase from above. She was wearing something glacial-blue and clingy, a wide sash at the waist, sapphire earrings, high-heeled pumps to match the dress. Blonde hair pulled back from the pale oval of her face. Blue eye shadow. No lipstick.

"You caught me at a bad time," she said. "I was dressing."

"Who's Mickey?" he asked.

"An acquaintance. I just called to say I'd be running late. I hope this won't take too long. Would you like a drink?"

14

The offer surprised him. You didn't hand a man his hat and offer him a drink in the same breath.

"Or are you still on duty?" she asked.

"Sort of."

"At eight-fifteen?"

"Long day," he said.

"Name your poison," she said, and for a moment he thought she was making a deliberate if somewhat grisly joke, but she was heading obliviously for the bar unit across the room.

"Scotch," he said.

"Ah, he's corruptible," she said, and turned to glance over her shoulder, smiling. "Anything with it?"

"Ice, please."

He watched her as she dropped ice cubes into two short glasses, poured scotch for him, gin for herself. He watched her as she carried the drink to where he was sitting. Pale horse, pale rider, pale good looks.

"Come sit by the fire," she said, "it'll be cozier," and started across the room toward a sofa upholstered in the same red crushed velvet. He rose, moved toward the sofa, waited for her to sit, and then sat beside her. She crossed her legs. There was a quick glimpse of nylon-sleek knees, the suggestion of a thigh, and then she lowered her skirt as demurely as a nun. In an almost subliminal flash, he wondered why she had chosen a word like "cozier."

"Mickey who?" he asked.

"Mouse," she said, and smiled again.

"A *male* acquaintance then."

"No, I was making a joke. Mickey's a girlfriend.

15

We're going out to dinner." A look at her watch. "Provided we're through here before midnight. I said I'd call her back."

"I won't be long," he said.

"So," she said. "What's so urgent?"

"Not urgent," he said.

"Pressing then?"

"Not pressing, either. Just a few things bothering me."

"Like what?"

"Your friends."

"Tom, Dick, and Harry?" she asked, and smiled again.

She was making reference to their first, somewhat irritating, meeting, but she was making sport of it now, seeming deliberately trying to put him at ease. He thought at once that he was being conned. And this led to the further thought that she had something to hide.

"I'm talking about the list you gave us," he said. "The men you consider close friends."

"Yes, they are," she said.

"Yes, so they told me." He paused. "That's what's bothering me."

"What is it, exactly, that's bothering you, Mr. Willis?" She shifted her weight on the sofa, adjusted her skirt again.

"Nelson Riley," he said. "Chip Endicott. Basil Hollander."

"Yes, yes, I know the names."

Basil Hollander was the man who'd left a message

16

on her answering machine saying he had tickets for the Philharmonic. His comments to Willis were echoes of what Nelson Riley and Chip Endicott had already told him. He considered Marilyn Hollis one of his very best friends. Terrific girl. Great fun to be with. But Hollander (who'd identified himself as "Baz" on Marilyn's answering machine) was a "Yes-No-Well" respondent, the kind detectives the world over dreaded. Getting him to amplify was like pulling teeth.

"Have you known her a long time?"

"Yes."

"How long?"

"Well ..."

"A year?"

"No."

"Longer?"

"No."

"Ten months?"

"No."

"Less than ten months?"

"Yes."

"Five months?"

"No."

"Less than ten months but more than five months?"

"Yes."

"Eight months?"

"Yes."

"How well did you know her?"

"Well ..."

"For example, were you sleeping with her?"

"Yes."

17

"Regularly?"

"No."

"Frequently?"

"No."

"Occasionally?"

"Yes."

"Do you know anyone named Jerry McKennon?"

"No."

And like that.

The thing that troubled Willis was that the men had sounded identical.

Taking into allowance their different verbal styles (Hollander, for example, had interrupted the questioning with a surprisingly eloquent and exuberant sidebar on a pianist Willis had never heard of), accepting, too, the differences in their life-styles and vocations (Hollander was an accountant, Riley a painter, Endicott a lawyer), and their ages (Endicott was fifty-seven, Riley thirty-eight or -nine, Hollander forty-two), taking all this into account, Willis nonetheless came away with the feeling that he could have tape-recorded his first conversation with Marilyn and saved himself the trouble of talking to the three men on her list.

We're very good friends, the lady had said.

We sleep together occasionally.

We have a lot of fun.

They do not know Jerry McKennon.

They do not know each other.

Yet three different men who did not know each other had defined their relationship with Marilyn Hollis exactly as she had described it. And each of them had

18

come up with substantial alibis for Sunday night and Monday morning—while McKennon was either killing himself or getting himself killed:

Nelson Riley was with the lady in Vermont on Sunday night—or so he'd said. He was still there on Monday morning, taking a few final runs with her on icy slopes before starting the long drive back to the city.

Chip Endicott was at a Bar Association dinner on Sunday night, and at his desk bright and early Monday morning.

On Sunday night, Hollander had been to a chamber music recital at Randall Forbes Hall in the Springfield Center complex downtown. On Monday morning at eight o'clock, while McKennon was presumably gasping his life out to an answering machine, Hollander was on the subway, commuting to his job at the accounting offices of Kiley, Benson, Marx, and Rudolph.

All present and accounted for.

But Willis could not shake the feeling that he'd seen the same play three different times, with three different people playing the same character and repeating the playwright's lines in their own individual acting styles.

Had Marilyn Hollis been the playwright?

Had she picked up the phone the moment the detectives left her and told Nelson, Chip, Baz—mustn't forget old taciturn Baz—that the police were just there, and she'd appreciate it if they said they were dear good buddies who never heard of anyone named Jerry McKennon, thanks a lot, catch you in the sack sometime.

But if so—why?

Her alibi was airtight.

But so were the others.

If only they hadn't sounded so very much alike.

Well, look, maybe the relationships *were* identical. Maybe Marilyn Hollis defined the exact course a "friendship" would take and God help the poor bastard who strayed an inch from that prescribed path.

Maybe.

"Tell me more about them," he said.

"There's nothing more to tell," she said, "they're good friends."

And then, suddenly and unexpectedly: "Have you ever killed anyone?"

He looked at her, surprised.

"Why do you ask?"

"Just curious."

He hesitated a moment, and then said, "Yes."

"How did it feel?"

"I thought *I* was asking the questions," he said.

"Oh, the hell with the questions," she said. "I've already talked to all three of them, I know exactly what you said and exactly what they said, so why go through it all over again? You're here because they all gave you the same story, isn't that right?"

This time he blinked.

"Isn't it?"

"Well . . . yes," he said.

"Now you sound like Baz," she said, and laughed. "I adore him, he's such a sweetheart," she said. "I adore them all, they're *such* good friends."

"So they said."

"Yes, I *know* what they said. And you think they

were lying, that I rehearsed them, whatever. But why would I have done that? And isn't it entirely possible that we think of each other *exactly* that way? As very good friends? All of us? Separately?"

"I suppose."

"Do *you* have any good friends, Mr. Willis?"

"Yes."

"Who?"

"Well . . ."

"Ah, there's Baz again."

"I have friends," he said, and wondered about it for the first time.

"Who? Cops?"

"Yes."

"Women cops?"

"Some of them."

"Who are friends?"

"Well . . . I don't think any of the women cops I know are . . . well . . . what you'd call friends, no."

"Then what? Lovers?"

"No, none of the women I see are cops."

"Do you have any women friends at *all*? Women you could actually call friends?"

"Well . . ."

"You do a very good Baz imitation, Mr. Willis. Do I have to keep calling you Mr. Willis? What's your first name?"

"Harold."

"Is that what your friends call you?"

"They call me Hal."

"May I call you Hal?"

21

"Well . . ."

"Oh, come on, I didn't for Christ's sake *murder* him! Relax, will you? Enjoy your scotch, enjoy the fire, call me Marilyn, *relax*!"

"Well . . ."

"Hal?" she said.

"Yes?"

"Relax, Hal."

"I'm relaxed," he said.

"No, you're not relaxed. I know when a man is relaxed, and you're not relaxed. You're very tense. Because you think I murdered Jerry and you're sure that's why I offered you a drink and the comfort of my fire, isn't that right?"

"Well . . ."

"If you want to be my friend, be honest with me, will you please? I hate phonies. Even if they're cops."

He was looking at her in open astonishment now. He took a quick swallow of scotch and then—to reassure himself that he was a working cop with some serious questions to ask—immediately said, "Well, you have to admit it was sort of funny, getting the same playback from three different . . ."

"Not at all," she said. "None of them would know *how* to lie, that's why they're my friends. That's what we enjoy with each other, Hal. Relationships that are entirely free of bullshit. Have you ever had such a relationship in your life?"

"Well . . . no. I guess not."

"You're missing something. Would you like another drink?"

"I know you've got a date . . ."

"She can wait," Marilyn said, and rose from the couch. "Same thing?"

"Please," Willis said, and handed her his glass.

He watched her as she moved toward the bar.

"Are you looking at my ass?" she said.

"Well . . ."

"If you are, then say so."

"Well, I was. Until you mentioned it."

She came back to him with the drink. She handed him the glass and sat down beside him. "Tell me about the man you killed," she said.

"It wasn't a man," Willis said.

He hadn't talked about this in a long long time. Nor did he want to talk about it now.

"A woman then."

"No."

"What does that leave?"

"Forget it," he said. He swallowed most of the scotch in his glass, rose, and then said, "Miss Hollis, I know you're busy, so maybe it'd be best if I . . ."

"Scared?" she said.

"No, not particularly."

"Then sit down."

"Why?"

"Because I like talking to you. And talking is the way people begin."

He looked at her.

"What is this?" he said.

"What *is* it? What is *what*?"

"I walk in here off the street . . ."

23

"Yes . . ."

"You spit fire the first time we meet . . ."

"That was the first time."

"So now . . ."

"So now sit down and talk to me."

"Your girlfriend's expecting you to . . ."

"Who'd you kill?" Marilyn said.

He kept looking at her.

"Sit down," she said. "Please."

He said nothing.

"Let me freshen that," she said, and took his nearly empty glass. He did not sit. Instead, he watched her again as she went to the bar, and half-filled two water tumblers, one with scotch, the other with gin.

He did not want to talk about who the hell he'd killed or didn't kill. He looked at her ass instead. He hoped she wouldn't ask again if he was looking at her ass, and was relieved when she didn't. She came back to him, handed him the scotch, and then sat again. Nylon-sleek knees again. No tug at the skirt this time. He did not sit beside her.

"Sit," she said, and patted the sofa. "Who'd you kill, Hal?"

"Why do you want to know?"

"Honesty," she said, and shrugged.

He hesitated.

"Tell me," she said.

The fire crackled and spit. A log shifted on the grate.

"Tell me, Hal," she said.

He took a deep breath.

"A boy," he said.

"What?"

"He was a boy."

"How old?"

"Twelve."

"Jesus," she said softly.

"With a .357 Magnum in his fist."

"When was this?"

"Long ago."

"How long ago?"

"I was a rookie cop."

"Was he white or black?"

"Black."

"Which made it worse."

"Nothing could have made it worse," he said.

"I meant . . ."

"I know what you meant. There was that, yes, but . . . you see, that wasn't what mattered to me . . . I mean, what the newspapers were saying, white cop kills innocent black kid . . . he was coming off a robbery, he'd just killed three people inside a liquor store, but that wasn't . . . I had to shoot him, it would've been me in the next three seconds. But . . . he was twelve years old."

"God," she said.

Almost a whisper.

"Yeah," he said. "That was the thing."

"How awful for you," she said.

"Yeah," he said again.

Silence.

He wondered why he was telling her this.

Well, honesty, he thought.

"His mother . . . his mother came to the police station," he said, his voice very low now. "And she . . . she asked the sergeant where she could find Patrolman Willis . . . they called us patrolmen in those days, now they call the blues police officers . . . and I was just coming in from downtown where I'd been answering questions at Headquarters all morning, and the sergeant said, 'There he is, lady,' not realizing, not knowing she was the boy's mother, and she came up to me and . . . and . . . spit in my face. Didn't say anything. Just spit in my face and walked out. I stood there . . . I . . . there were guys all around . . . a muster room is a busy place . . . and I . . . I guess I . . . I guess I began crying."

He shrugged.

And fell silent again.

She was watching his face.

Two shots in the chest, he thought.

Kept coming.

Another shot in the head.

Caught him between the eyes.

Questions afterward. Two big bulls from Homicide. Confusion and noise. Some guy from one of the local television stations trying to get a camera inside the liquor store there, take some pictures of the carnage. The owner and two women lying dead on the floor, smashed whiskey bottles all around them. The kid outside on the sidewalk with his brains blown out.

Ah, shit, he thought.

This city, he thought, this goddamn fucking city.

"Are you all right?" Marilyn asked.

"Yes," he said.

"You haven't touched your scotch."

"I guess I haven't."

She lifted her own glass. "Here's to golden days and purple nights," she said, and clinked the glass against his.

He nodded, said nothing.

"That was my father's favorite toast," she said. "How old are you, Hal?"

"Thirty-four," he said.

"How old were you when it happened?"

He took a swallow of scotch and then said, "Twenty-two." He shook his head. "He'd just killed three people inside that liquor store. The owner and two ladies."

"I would have done just what you did," Marilyn said.

"Well . . ." Willis said, and shrugged again. "If only he'd put down the gun . . ."

"But he didn't . . ."

"I *told* him to put it down, I warned him . . ." He shook his head again. "He just kept coming at me."

"So you shot him."

"Yes."

"How many times?"

"Three times," Willis said.

"That's a lot of times."

"Yes."

They both fell silent. Willis sipped at the scotch. Marilyn kept watching him.

"You're small for a cop," she said.

"I know. Five-eight."

27

"Most cops are bigger. Detectives especially. Not that I ever *met* a detective before now. I mean in the movies. Most of them are very big."

"Well, the movies," Willis said.

"You never killed anybody before that, huh?"

"No."

"Wow," she said, and fell silent for several moments. At last, she said, "What time is it?"

He looked at his watch. "Almost nine," he said.

"I really have to call Mickey," she said. "I'm sorry, I don't mean to rush you out."

"That's okay," he said, "I've taken enough of your time."

"Well, finish your drink," she said. "And if you want my advice, you'll put the whole thing out of your mind, really. You killed a man, okay, but that's not such a big deal. Really. Do you understand what I'm saying?"

He nodded and said nothing.

He was thinking: Not a man, a boy.

He drained the scotch. He was feeling warm and a bit light-headed. He put the empty glass down on the coffee table.

"Thanks for the drink," he said. "Drinks."

"So where do you go now?" she asked.

"Back to the office, type up the reports."

"Will I see you again?"

Still sitting, looking up at him, pale eyes studying his. He hesitated.

"I didn't kill Jerry," she said.

Eyes fastened to his.

28

"Call me," she said.

He said nothing.

"Will you?"

"If you want me to," he said.

"I want you to."

"Then I will," he said, and shrugged.

"Let me get your coat," she said, and rose, sleek knees flashing.

"I can find my way out," he said. "I know you're in a hurry."

"Don't be silly," she said.

She took his coat from the rack and helped him into it. Just before he went out, she said, "Call me, don't forget."

"I'll call," he said.

The wind hit him the minute he stepped outside, dispelling alcohol and cozy fire, yanking him back to reality. He walked across to where he'd parked the car, struggled with a frozen lock, held a match under the key and finally managed to open the door. He started the car and turned on the heater. He wiped his gloved hand over the frost-rimed windshield.

He did not know why he decided to sit there in the car, watching her building across the street.

Maybe he'd just been a detective for too long a time.

Twenty minutes later, a black 280 SEL Mercedes-Benz pulled up to the curb in front of Marilyn's building. Willis watched as the door on the curb side opened.

Her girlfriend Mickey, he thought.

Better late than never.

29

Mickey—if that's who it was—locked the car door, walked the few steps to Marilyn's building, took off a glove, and pressed the bell button.

A moment later, Mickey—if that's who it was—opened the door and went inside.

Mickey—if that's who it was—was a six-foot-three-inch-tall, two-hundred-and-twenty-pound male white Caucasian wearing a bulky raccoon coat that made him look even bigger than he was.

Honesty, the lady had said.

Bullshit, Willis thought, and jotted down the license-plate number and then drove back to the station house to type up his reports in triplicate.

Busman's Holiday

JOSH PACHTER

Josh Pachter, an instructor in the University of Maryland's European Division in West Germany, is well known to mystery fans for his stories and parodies in various magazines and for his anthology Top Crime (1985).

He writes a column on short stories for Mystery Scene *and is currently working on his first novel. Janwillem van de Wetering's story "There Goes Ravelaar," nominated for an Edgar in 1968, was translated from Dutch into English by Mr. Pachter.*

FRIDAY, EARLY JUNE. Late afternoon. Outside the window of Busman's ninth-floor Washington office, fleecy clouds punctuate a pale-blue sky. A cheerful songbird hops around on the windowsill making music barely audible through the hum of the air-conditioning.

Busman sits in a leather swivel chair behind his huge

oak desk, restless. It's almost time to pack it in, just finish up a few last items of paperwork and go.

Jackson's expense account for that damned fiasco in New York. Obviously padded, but what the hell? It's too nice a day to grouch. Busman scribbles his initials and drops the form in his OUT basket.

Weekly progress report. He reads it through for typos. There aren't any. Busman chuckles. Leave it to Theresa! He signs at the bottom of the second and final sheet, slips both pages into an Interdepartmental Communication envelope, scrawls the Chief's name and drops the envelope atop the other papers in his OUT basket.

Purchase orders, disbursements, two interesting new contracts. Initial, sign, and OUT.

Busman glances at his wristwatch. It's five o'clock. He glances at his desk. He's all finished.

He smiles, stands, stretches happily. Grabs his hat and coat.

In the outer office, buxom, blue-eyed Theresa is still pecking away diligently at her word processor. Sexy Terry, the secretary. Some joke. Some secretary!

She looks up from her keyboard with a friendly smile and a twinkle in those lovely eyes. "Leaving, Mr. Busman?"

He nods.

"Well, I'll see you in two weeks, then. You have a great time, now, hear?"

Busman returns her smile. "Thanks, Terry. I will. Don't let 'em work you too hard while I'm gone."

A crowded elevator deposits him in the lobby, and

32

he swings through the revolving door into the warm summer sunshine. On the sidewalk, Busman stops for a moment and draws in a deep, satisfied breath. Invigorated, he strolls the four blocks crosstown. He enjoys the walk.

With a thin line of perspiration beginning to form on his upper lip, Busman ransoms his car from the underground parking garage where he leaves it every working morning and slaps two quarters into the young attendant's outstretched palm. A silly convention, tipping, but a guy's got to make a buck any way he can these days.

Busman slides behind the wheel of his year-old T-Bird, drops it into drive and inches up to the sidewalk. A fat old woman in a flowered housedress waddles past his windshield, bulging shopping bags clutched in her fists. She is muttering angrily, wildly, though there is no one near enough to hear her. When she is gone, Busman shakes his head, looks both ways, and edges out into the rush-hour traffic.

He crawls to the first red light, waits impatiently, then crawls on to the next one. Traffic, traffic, traffic.

Well, hell, what's the rush? It's a beautiful day, he's got two weeks' vacation to look forward to. Take it easy, tiger.

The radio, maybe? Sure, there you go. He leans over and switches it on. No, not that New Wave noise. Something soothing, without the green hair and razor blades. He tunes in a different station. Ah, better. Muted strings. Nice.

The air-conditioning's been cranky lately, so he

33

cracks open the window. A gentle breeze whispers in, teases the graying hairs at the back of his neck. Very nice.

Finally, Busman crosses out of the District and into Maryland. He works his way through Bethesda, then gets onto I-70 heading northwest. The traffic loosens up; his right foot feeds gas to the T-Bird's powerful engine; the speedometer needle moves to 60 and stays there for half an hour. When the sign for Frederick comes into view, he hits his blinker and changes over to the right-hand lane. He slows down and leaves the highway, turns right at the head of the exit ramp. Takes the third left, the second right, the second right again.

Ahead, at the end of Wisteria Lane, he spots a long black LeMans in his driveway. Busman frowns, wondering, *What am I, early?* But no, the dashboard clock reads 6:15 and his wristwatch agrees. Romero must be running behind schedule. Well, thinks Busman, can't really blame the bastard. He's probably trying to squeeze two weeks' worth into one last afternoon.

Busman sighs, swings into a three-point turn and heads back in the direction of the highway. He doesn't get on it, though. He drives straight ahead, under the overpass, to a little shopping plaza a mile down the road. The place is crowded at this hour and he has to park a half-dozen doors down from the luncheonette. Inside, he dawdles over a cup of coffee and a cinnamon Danish, kids around pleasantly with the waitress. A high school kid with a nice shape to her but freckles. Her name tag reads Randye. Pretty girl.

At 6:40 he pays his bill, leaves a quarter for Randye,

and drives back home. The black LeMans is gone from his driveway, and a tight smile crosses his lips as he puts his car in the garage next to Julia's station wagon.

The front door is unlocked, and Busman finds his wife in the dining room setting the still-beautiful rosewood table they bought on their honeymoon in Montreal, almost twenty years ago. She, too, is still beautiful, and Busman admires how carefully she is dressed, her makeup fresh, not a hair out of place. Interesting, he thinks. Commendable.

A small woman, she stands on tiptoe to touch his cheek with her painted lips. "Hello, darling. You're a little late."

"Mmm," he says. "Stopped for coffee on the way."

"Oh?" Is that a flicker of relief washing across her face? Maybe. Maybe. "Dinner'll be ready in a few minutes. Would you like a drink?"

And Busman's vacation begins. Julia serves Cornish hens with an elaborate salad and a bottle of Bernkasteler Riesling. An *Auslese,* which goes well with the meal. After coffee, they spend the evening quietly, Busman with the *Post* and Julia with her knitting. Their conversation is sporadic and harmonious. They go to sleep early in separate beds, an arrangement of long standing. The sexual attraction that first drew them together, during their sophomore year at Georgetown in the early sixties, faded more than a decade ago.

The next morning, Busman sleeps in. He rises at half past nine, showers and shaves slowly, and slips into faded jeans and an "I ♡ DC" T-shirt instead of his usual jacket and tie. He eats a leisurely breakfast of bacon and eggs, a welcome switch from his usual hurried toast and coffee.

All morning, he putters about happily in the garden behind his house. Plant, water, prune, pamper. His snap beans are doing surprisingly well, but he's a little worried about his tomatoes. Julia stays indoors, busy with laundry and the vacuuming and lunch. They eat on the patio, chicken enchiladas and cold Dos Equis. While Julia clears the dishes from the redwood picnic table, Busman goes back to his garden.

And day melts into night.

After dinner they settle down in the living room, Busman in his favorite armchair with last month's bestseller, bought then but not opened until now, Julia with her needles and yarn. The television plays softly, but neither of them pays much attention to it. Page 50. Page 100. Page 150. The garment Julia is working on begins to look something like a sweater. Around 10:30, Busman looks up from his book and catches his wife's eye and smiles.

And night melts back to day. . . .

A week passes. A good, restful week.

Then, late one afternoon, while Busman is trying to decide whether or not his lettuce are far enough apart, the telephone rings. He stands up and brushes dirt from his hands.

"I've got it," calls Julia from inside the house. The ringing is sliced off as she lifts the receiver.

Some office crisis? Busman waits for her shouted "It's for you, dear!" But a minute goes by and the house is silent. He frowns. He shrugs. He kneels. His

36

hands work into the soft, rich soil, and grass stains work deeper into the knees of his trousers.

On the horizon, the sun is an immense ball of fire, sinking. . . .

The next morning at breakfast, Julia announces a shopping trip. "Need anything, darling?"

"No. Nothing." Busman sops up the last drops of egg yolk with a triangle of toast.

"Want another cup of coffee?"

"No, thanks."

"I'll be back in a couple of hours."

"Mmm."

She leans over and pecks his cheek. When she leaves, the sound of the front door swinging shut behind her is loud in the empty house.

Busman lifts his cup and drains it. There is a grim half-smile on his face.

So, today's the day. . . .

He gets up, stacks the dishes in the sink and goes out to his garden.

An hour later he checks his watch. Yes, now. He puts his tools away neatly and goes back inside. He picks up the telephone handset and dials a memorized number.

"Hello?"

"Busman here, Vito. Let's go."

"Yes, sir. Give me fifteen minutes to get there."

"Check."

Neither man hangs up. If anyone should call while he's gone, the line will be busy. Later, just in case, Vito

37

can testify to a lengthy business conversation. A reliable witness. An iron-clad alibi. Just what the doctor ordered.

In the tiled bathroom upstairs, Busman scrubs his face and hands. When he is finished, he examines his fingernails closely. They are clean, no dirt from his garden shows. He shaves, then, and changes into a brand-new pearl-gray suit, a somber tie, a new pair of shoes bought half a size too large. Just in case.

He slides open the bottom drawer of his dresser. Beneath a pile of outgrown sweaters he feels the cool metal of a gun and silencer. He draws them forth and breaks open the gun. It is loaded. He screws the silencer onto the barrel and slips the weapon into the right-hand pocket of his suit coat.

Got everything? He pats his trouser pockets and feels the duplicate key he had made from Julia's own, the handkerchief, the thin cotton gloves. He checks his wallet and confirms that the gun registration is there.

That's it, then.

He leaves the house by the back door. At the low property fence separating his yard from his neighbors' he checks to make sure that no one is watching. He hops the fence and cuts across to the next block. As usual at this hour of the morning, the neighborhood is deserted: husbands are off at work and children at school, wives are inside with the curtains drawn and the air conditioners on, escaping the heat and humidity. A small Italian sports car is waiting for him, a stocky Mediterranean type in nondescript shirt and slacks at the wheel. Busman gets in, and the car pulls smoothly away from the curb. No words are exchanged between passenger and driver.

The ride takes twenty minutes, first north, then east. At last they pull up before a compact ranch house set well back from a lonely country lane. Unimpressive, but a safe trysting place. There is a long black LeMans in the driveway, and Julia's station wagon is parked beside it. The driver shifts into neutral and leaves his engine running.

Busman looks up and down the street. It is empty. "Be right back," he says, and unfolds his six-foot frame from the little sports car and walks briskly to the front door of the house. He draws on his thin white gloves as he walks, and noiselessly lets himself into Romero's house with his duplicate key.

Standing in the foyer facing three closed doors, the builder's blueprint he has studied clicks into place in Busman's mind. Living room, kitchen, bedroom. Yes, that one.

He steps softly to the door and listens. He hears faint murmurings from within. Love sounds.

Busman's face hardens; his black eyes chill. Straightening, he pulls the silenced gun from his pocket. He draws a deep breath and holds it.

Now.

He twists the smooth brass doorknob and swings the door open and moves swiftly forward.

The naked figures on the double bed spring apart. There is horror in Julia's eyes. Romero's face is a mask.

"Get up, Romero."

"No, listen, Busman. I—"

39

"Get up!"

Romero swings his legs over the side of the bed, pulling the rumpled top sheet around him to cover his nakedness. "Calm down, now, Busman. Put the gun away. Can't we—"

"Talk things over? Be reasonable?" Busman chuckles. "No."

"You're not going to—?" There is a pronounced tremor in his voice. "What are you going to do?"

"I said get up."

Romero stands. The sheet falls away as he rises. His cock is small, shriveled, as if it's trying to hide from the gun.

Busman takes a step closer to the bed and issues orders. "Get over to your desk. Sit down. Take out one sheet of stationery and a pen. Not that drawer, Romero! You think I don't know what's in there? Try the top drawer. Good. Now write what I tell you: 'It all happened so fast. One minute it was just another argument, the next minute—' "

"Busman!" Romero is pleading now, cowering in his straight-backed wooden chair. "You're crazy! You can't—"

Busman jabs the gun toward him. " '—the next minute it was over. What do I do now? I don't really have much choice.' Now sign your name."

"Busman!"

"*Sign it!*"

Romero signs. The pen is in his right hand: another detail checks.

"All right, now back to bed. Move it!"

Busman crosses the room to Romero's desk and checks the note. Yes, perfect. The handwriting is shaky, nervous. Natural enough, for a murderer about to commit suicide.

Finally Julia speaks. "Don't." A whisper. "Please." Barely audible. "Please don't."

"For Christ's sake, Busman, you can't do this! You'll never get away with it! I—it's not my gun! They'll trace it back to you!"

Busman takes his wallet from his hip pocket and slides out the light-green registration slip. "It *is* yours," he says. "Bought and registered in your name a month ago, according to this. I think your signature turned out nicely." Without looking away from the man in the bed, he buries the document among the other papers in the drawer of the spindly night table.

A final step closer. Busman holds the gun to the right side of Romero's head.

"Busman, you—"

Is the angle correct for a suicide? Yes.

"Busman!"

Busman pulls the trigger. There is a breathy *pfffft*, like an arrow whizzing by overhead.

Romero falls back on his pillow. There is blood everywhere.

Busman turns to his wife. She is staring at the body lying next to her, her eyes are wide with horror.

Busman smiles reassuringly and walks around the perimeter of the double bed to approach her. She shrinks away from him, tries to scream, but he claps his left hand over her mouth, holding her in a modified

41

headlock, and draws her closer. She struggles uselessly against his strength.

Busman touches the cold end of the silencer to her breast. Her body jerks taut at the feel of it, strains, then slumps in the recognition of defeat. She whimpers softly, like a wounded animal. Busman would like to stroke her cheek for a moment, to give her a moment of kindness, but he is holding her in place with his left hand and the gun is in his right. "If only I could trust you, Julia," he explains.

Her lips move wordlessly against his fingers. Her deep brown eyes contain a plea.

Busman sighs, and gently squeezes the trigger.

Pfffft.

The bedroom becomes quiet.

He unscrews the silencer and slips it back in his jacket pocket. He wipes the gun clean with his handkerchief and presses it into Romero's right hand.

Busman glances around the room. Everything is set. The note and the gun registration are in place, Romero and Julia are on the bed.

Hey, Romero and Julia. The star-crossed lovers. He's never thought of that before. He chuckles. Some joke. Some lovers.

Busman goes back out to the hallway, eases the front door open a crack and checks outside. The coast is clear. He sprints to the sports car at the curb and gets in. Without a word, the driver pumps the clutch and shifts into gear and drives off. Twenty minutes later they are back at the pickup point, a block from home.

For the first time, Busman hears his driver's voice.

42

"What about those clothes, sir? Do you want me to get rid of them for you?"

He frowns and makes a mental note. There was no need for such an offer; this man has not been adequately briefed. "No," he says, "that's all been arranged. Thanks." He climbs out of the car and it wheels away, around the corner and out of sight.

Busman cuts through his neighbors' yard, jumps the fence and goes back into his house. He sees no one, is seen by no one, just as planned. He picks up the telephone. "Vito?"

"Right here, Mr. Busman. How'd it go?"

"Fine. Some blood on my suit. No problem." He is about to say something about the driver's unnecessary comment, but decides against it. What the hell, it's too nice a day to grouch. "How long have I been gone?"

"Less than an hour."

Less than an hour. Excellent. "If the police have any questions, I may be giving them your number."

"Yes, sir, I know. I'll be ready. Good luck."

"Thanks." Busman hangs up the phone. Upstairs, he showers and changes back into jeans and a T-shirt. He carries his topcoat and bloodstained garments out behind the house and dumps them in the metal oil drum he burns fallen leaves in every autumn, along with the cotton gloves and the handkerchief and the too-big shoes. Things have changed in this community. Used to be a man could burn leaves, do whatever he wanted in the privacy of his own yard, without the township getting all in an uproar about it, but nowadays you need a permit. Busman has one—and a real one, for this, not a phony. He fills the oil drum with the pile of pruned branches he has left out in the sun to dry, then pours kerosene and strikes a match. He stands back and watches the blaze. Half an hour later he wrestles the drum over to the patio and upends it, stirs up the ashes and washes them away with the garden hose.

When the oil drum is back in its place, he carefully digs up a young sapling just this side of the property fence. At the bottom of the hole he places the silencer, the duplicate key to Romero's house, the fused zipper from his incinerated pants, the melted plastic from his suit and topcoat buttons. He covers the refuse over with a layer of rich soil and replants the sapling. Satisfied, he shoves his trowel into the earth and sighs a long, contented sigh.

Finished.

He gets to his feet and walks slowly up to the house. At the back door he stops, shakes his head and tsks his tongue against the roof of his mouth.

He goes back to the fence and retrieves his trowel, and puts it away with the rest of the gardening tools.

That's better.

Now for a beer.

Early that evening, Busman is sitting in his armchair with a glass of scotch in his hand and the stereo whispering when the telephone rings.

"Hello?"

"This Mr. Busman speaking?"

"Yes, who's this?"

"Yeah, well, my name's Detective-Lieutenant Herskowitz, Mr. Busman. Carroll County Police."

"Police?" Busman allows a note of apprehensive curiosity to color his voice, but is careful not to overdo it.

"Yeah, right." Then it comes. Afraid I've got some bad news for you. Really sorry to have to break it like this, but—

What? *What?* No, that's impossible, officer. No, she —what? Oh, Jesus, are you sure? Are you sure it's her? What? Yes, yes, of course. Where is it? All right, I'm leaving right now, I'll be there as soon as I can get there. Yes. Yes, I will. All right. Yes.

He hangs up the phone and tosses off the last half-inch of his drink, then goes out to the T-Bird and drives thirty minutes to the Carroll County Morgue.

The officers there are uncomfortable yet sympathetic. Detective-Lieutenant Herskowitz leads him to a small, dim viewing room. There are two wheeled dollies in the room, and on each of them a crisp white bedsheet covers a motionless human form. A solemn attendant pulls the sheet away from one of the faces. It is Julia. Busman gasps. "Oh, Christ, yes, that's her."

What? The other body? No, really, Officer, I'd really rather not. What's that? Her *what?* You must be— no, I don't believe it. We were perfectly happy together, I'd have known if she was having an affair. I don't—what? Well, yes, all right, then, if you really think it's necessary. My God, that's awful! What? Jesus Christ, Officer, how am I supposed to know if

45

I've ever seen him before? Half his damn head's been blown away! Who? Romero? No, I don't . . . I'm sorry, no, I've never heard of him. You say Julia was—my wife was—

No one even asks him for an alibi. Herskowitz offers to drive him home, but he demurs. "No, thanks," he says. "I—I'll manage."

Back home, Busman pours himself a tall scotch over lots of ice. He throws together a salad for supper and douses it with the bottled Thousand Island dressing which, although he's never had the heart to admit this to Julia, he prefers over the homemade stuff it took her half an hour to prepare from scratch. After dinner he switches on the television and catches most of an old Frank Capra film with Jimmy Stewart and Donna Reed. It's a Christmas story, and he can't figure out why they're showing it in June. He's seen it before, more than once, but he cries at the end of it anyway. He always does.

There is nothing about the Carroll County murder-suicide on the eleven o'clock news. David Letterman is sitting in for Johnny on the "Tonight Show," and Busman does not think his opening monologue is particularly funny. He turns off the set and goes to bed.

And his vacation resumes. He takes three hours away from his gardening to attend Julia's funeral. There are cards and phone calls from assorted friends and relatives. Otherwise, it is a quiet time.

Six days later, he goes back to work. As he enters his outer office, Theresa looks up from her word processor. "Mr. Busman!" Her blue eyes fill with mist. "I didn't think you'd—I—I was so sorry to hear about—about your wife." A single tear trickles down her cheek. "If there's anything I can do for you, really, anything at all . . ."

Sexy Terry, the secretary.

Busman murmurs thanks and brushes sadly past her into the inner office. He trees his hat and sits behind his desk. His IN basket is close to overflowing, but first things first. He unlocks the top desk drawer and digs out the note from the Chief and reads it over.

"Busman," it says, "Romero's thugs have intercepted our last two shipments of blow. He's got to be stopped. From things I hear, you may want to handle this one personally. Why don't you take a few weeks off and deal with it at your leisure? Thanks."

A thought strikes him, and he leans back in his chair and chuckles.

Busman's holiday.

He hasn't thought of that before.

Some joke.

Some holiday.

Little Moses/ The Society for the Reclamation and Restoration of "E. Auguste Napoléon Bonaparte"

JOYCE CAROL OATES

"Little Moses" is an excerpt from a novel in progress, planned for publication in 1988 or 1989, which will complete a quintet of what Miss Oates calls "American genre novels." She has provided a description of the work from which the story that follows is taken: "My Heart Laid Bare is a mock-memoir chronicling the fortunes and misfortunes of a family of confidence men named Licht. It begins in colonial America and ends with the election of FDR in 1932. In these selections the father of the clan, Abraham Licht, works a particularly ingenious con with his adopted (black) son Elisha. 'No crime without complicity,' is Abraham Licht's watchword, '—and, with complicity, no crime.'"

I.   Little Moses

CRIME? WHISPERS FATHER.
Then complicity.
Complicity?
Then no crime.

"Little Moses," husky for a child of ten, isn't he, sweet-tempered and dim-witted, obedient, faithful, uncomplaining, yes, black as pitch, yes, able and willing to do the work of a near-grown man, and, yes, he will grow, and grow, and grow, and he will work, and work, and work, and, being sweet of temper and dim of wit and black, black as pitch, he is faithful as a dog, he will be loyal for life, he has no *thought* of anything save work, he has no *thoughts* as you and I do, as white folks do, and, being of course the son, that is the grandson, of Alabama plantation slaves—will he not repay his cost numberless times over the next fifty years?

And his cost, sir, is so reasonable, sir, I will whisper it in your ear so that he cannot hear: six hundred dollars cash.

Lemuel Shattuck, farmer, of Black Eddy, Michigan; Alvah Gunness, farmer, of La Porte, Minnesota; Ole Budsberg, blacksmith, of Dryden, Minnesota; William Elias Schutt, candymaker, of Elbow Lake, Illinois; Jules Rulloff, farmer, of Horseheads, New York; the Abbotts, dairy farmers, of Lake Seneca, New York; the Wilmots, cotton manufacturers, of North Thetford, Pennsylvania. . . . *And his cost, sir, is so reasonable, sir,*

49

I will whisper it in your ear so that he cannot hear: six hundred dollars cash.

Though the prosperous Uriah Skillings, stable owner, of Glen Rapids, Ohio, paid $1,000. And Estes Morehouse, retired classicist, of Rocky Hill, New Jersey, paid $800.

For these gentlemen, and for some others, "Little Moses" strutted, and cavorted, and grinned, and rolled his white, white eyeballs, and sang:

> Come listen all you gals and boys
> I'm just from Tuck-y-hoe
> I'm goin' to sing a lee-tle song
> My name's Jim Crow!
>
> Weel about and turn about
> And do jis *so*
> Eb'ry time I weel about
> I jump Jim Crow!

In the autumn and winter of '98, through the spring of '99, they crisscrossed the countryside, frequently by night, frequently by back roads, Solon J. Berry and his obedient "Little Moses." Mr. Berry, possessed of a broad heavy melancholy face, close-trimmed salt-and-pepper whiskers, wire-rimmed glasses, a farmer who had lost his eighty-acre farm, a mill owner who had lost his mill, a former railroad agent for the Chesapeake & Ohio, a former druggist of Marion, Ohio, a casualty of the recession, once proud now humbled, once a man who owned property free and clear, now a man hounded by creditors, ashen skin, pouched eyes, queer nicks and blemishes in his cheeks, forced to certain actions, compromises, pragmatical measures which, in his prime, he would never have considered,—being a Christian, after all, of stolid Calvinist faith.

Solon J. Berry, or Whittaker Hale, or Hambleton Fogg, but always "Little Moses," for he was plucked from the bulrushes, yes, more or less, yes indeed, an Act of God, saved from certain drowning when the mighty Wabash River overflowed its banks in April '89 in Lafayette, Indiana, a howling black baby discovered amid drowned dogs, drowned chickens, drowned rats, snagged by an iron hook and pulled to shore, lifted from a nest of matted grass and filth that teemed with spiders, a living infant!—a black infant!—abandoned by his mother yet living, still, thrashing with life, mouth opened wide to howl, to shriek, a vast O of a mouth, wailing, wailing!—*why, the pitiful thing yet lives.*

And has grown husky, has he not?

And uncomplaining, and zealous, and patient, *and doesn't eat too much,* and can work twelve hours a day —farmwork, lifting and carrying, scouring pans, digging ditches, did I say twelve hours?—fourteen; sixteen; as many as a task requires. And doesn't need to sleep more than three, four hours, most nights, yes it is the black blood, yes his people were Alabama plantation slaves, the best West African stock, pitch-black, strong as horses, never sick a day until, at the age of

51

ninety-nine, they drop over dead, why that won't be till the year 2000, almost!—and here he is grinning, strutting, obedient as a puppy, clever as a little monkey, dull-witted as a sheep, reliable as an ox, and, when the mood is on him, a genuine entertainment right in the home, rolling his eyes, and snapping his fingers, and kicking up his heels, here is "Zip Coon," here is "Poor Black Boy," here is "Possum up a Gum Tree," but the *pièce de résistance*, the *ne plus ultra*, the *flagrante delicto*, stand back, give him room, it's wild "Jim Crow" himself . . . !

And all for $600. And no one ever to know, *precisely*, the terms of the orphan's contract.

Sometimes "Little Moses" slept for an hour or two in his new master's house, in a corner of the woodshed where rags had been tossed, in the back room in Grandpa's old urine-stained bed, once in a hayloft with mice and rats, once in a cardboard box beside a wood-burning stove whose embers smoldered with a slow dull cozy heat, sometimes, more often, "Little Moses" didn't risk sleep at all but lay awake, waiting, quietly waiting, for the white folks to settle down for the night.

Then he would slip away, not a creaking floorboard to betray him, not a barking dog, "Little Moses" running hunched-over, head down, crawling if need be, making his stealthy way from one shadowy area to the next, in case his new master was watching from a window (but how could he be watching, the fool was fast asleep with the rest), trotting out to the moonlit coun-

52

try road where, in the two-seater gig, "Solon J. Berry" waited, napping, as he liked to say, with one eye open.

"Is it true, Father," Elisha asked doubtfully, "—that you found me in the Wabash River?—*in a flood*?"

Abraham Licht smiled, and lay a warm protective hand on the boy's woolly hair, and said, after a pause of perhaps ten seconds, "No, 'Lisha. It was the Nautauga, back East, but folks hereabouts might not have heard of it; and I don't want to arouse their suspicions."

"Is it true, Father," Elisha asked, "—that the white folks is *devils*, and all of them *enemies*? Or is some of them different, like you?"

And Abraham Licht smiled, and sucked zestfully on his cigar, and said, "Now look here, 'Lisha,—*I'm not white*. I may look white, and I may talk white, but I stand outside the white race, just like you, and all of my people stand outside the white race, because they *are* devils, and they *are* our enemies, each and every one."

But none of the enemies reports Mr. Berry, or Mr. Hale, or Mr. Fogg to the police.

And none of the enemies reports "Little Moses" missing.

"Nor will they ever, the wretches!" Abraham Licht says, baring his big white teeth around his Cuban cigar, counting his cash, "—*that*, Baby Moses, we are assured of."

So they crisscross the countryside, keeping to the

53

back roads, upon occasion traveling fast,—very fast,—along a main artery,—no time to dally, no time to browse,—but for the most part ambling along in no great hurry: for the land *is* beautiful, the North American continent *is* beautiful: no matter (as Abraham Licht says with an upward twist of his lip) that human beings have begun to foul it.

(Does Elisha sometimes doubt that people, white *or* black, are devils?—and only the Lichts can be trusted?—Father then reads him tales from the newspapers, the confessions of the hard-hearted murderer Frank Abbott-Almy of Vermont, the "true story" of the monstrous Braxtons of Indiana, and, most ghastly of all, the saga of Widow Sorenson of Ohio, who acquired twenty-eight husbands by way of matrimonial journals, and, over a period of two decades, killed them for their money, and fed their remains to the hogs.

The lesson being, as Elisha learns to shape with his lips, while Father speaks: *All men are our enemies, then or now*; but, *brothers by blood are brothers by the soul.*)

Then one day Abraham Licht declares that he is *Licht* again, and Elisha is *Elisha*; and very suddenly he is homesick for Muirkirk; and his beloved Sophie; and dear little Millicent, whose seventh birthday,—*is* it the seventh?—he has missed, laboring here in the vineyards, casting his pearls before swine.

So, within an hour or two, he sells the two-seater gig, and the swayback horses, and buys some new clothes for himself and his boy, and arranges for them

54

to travel to Chautauqua in a private Pullman car, now he is Licht again, now he can breathe again, now he can hold his head high again, $4,500 in clear profits, $6,200, perhaps it is as much as $9,000, and not one of the enemies reports the affair to the police, not Shattuck, nor Gunness, nor Budsberg, nor Schutt, nor Rulloff, nor the Abbotts, nor the Wilmots, nor the others, the many others, the contemptible execrable *fools*, not a one! Not a one!

"And do you know why, 'Lisha?" Abraham asks.

'Lisha grins and nods; 'Lisha knows; in mock solemnity wheeling, and turning about, and mouthing the words, the terrible words, *I jump Jim Crow!*

II. The Society for the Reclamation and Restoration of "E. Auguste Napoléon Bonaparte"

In Corsvgate, in Allentown, in Bethlehem, Pennsylvania . . . in a scattering of suburbs and neighborhoods of Philadelphia . . . in New Jersey, in Sanford, Waterboro, Paterson, Elizabeth, and selected areas of Newark and New Brunswick . . . there began to appear, in the winter of 1912–13, a Mr. Gaymead, a Mr. Lichtman, a Mr. Bramhurst, "solicitors," as they called themselves, for the Wall Street brokerage firm authorized to represent, in North America, the secret Society for the Reclamation and Restoration of E. Auguste Napoléon Bonaparte.

"E. Auguste Napoléon Bonaparte"? The illegitimate son of the great Emperor, born in 1821, the year of the Emperor's death. And the lost heir to a great fortune.

(Which fortune has grown considerably since 1821, until, in the autumn of 1912, it is estimated to be in excess of $200 million—according to the confidential report of the prestigious New York accounting firm Hearns, Saddler.)

Messieurs Gaymead, Lichtman, and Bramhurst were all three gentlemen of stolid middle age, possessed of muttonchop whiskers (Gaymead), or flashing pince-nez (Lichtman), or a pencil-thin mustache (the balding Bramhurst); each dressed in Wall Street style, which is to say in a three-piece suit of a conservative, even austere, cut, though Mr. Bramhurst sometimes sported a white carnation in his buttonhole, and Mr. Lichtman, depending upon the occasion, sometimes wore a checked silk Ascot tie. One wore a signet ring on his smallest finger, another wore a gold watch chain; one cleared his throat officiously; another was in the lawyerly habit of gravely repeating his sentences, as if for a stenographer's ear. All three were completely devoted, above and beyond their salaries, to the (secret) Society for the Reclamation and Restoration of "E. Auguste Napoléon Bonaparte."

Inclined, perhaps, to be rather overpunctilious regarding such matters as birth certificates, genealogies, legal records, deeds of ownership of property, life insurance policies, savings accounts, and the like, these three "solicitors" could not resist now and then revealing their natural sympathies . . . for though the Society's negotiations were a matter of the highest confidentiality, and would, in time, provide descendants of Auguste Bonaparte with considerable sums of money (hundreds of thousands of dollars for some, as much as $1 million for others), it was nevertheless the case that Mr. Lichtman could not always resist informing a client about irregular steps being taken by certain not-to-be-named relatives of his, in advancing *their* claims to the inheritance; and Mr. Gaymead, though stiff and disconcertingly "British" in his manner, might sometimes break into a delighted smile when surprised by a client's especially perceptive remark.

Stout, balding Mr. Bramhurst, never one to raise false hopes, felt that he would rather err on the side of doubt, than inspire in his clients an unreasonable hope that the lawsuit might be settled soon. Authorized to pass along the president's words, in effect, Bramhurst would tell a small roomful of his clients that the legal situation in which the Society found itself was unparalleled in the history of inheritance claims. "But we will not rest until Napoléon Bonaparte's rightful heir is restored to his legitimacy, and the hundreds of millions of francs,—that is, *dollars*—honestly divided among his descendants; not for purposes of crass mercenary gain, but for reasons of honor. 'Honor is the subject of my story,' as the great Bard has said," Bramhurst would declare, stroking his mustache, and fixing his steel-gray eyes upon his listeners' faces. "Yet I must state sub-rosa that the French are no less duplicitous

57

at the present time than they were in 1821, when so many efforts were made to murder the infant Auguste, by agents of the 'legitimate' son and Louis Napoléon alike; and it is hardly a secret that their civilization has, in the past century, lapsed into extreme decadence . . . which only war, I am afraid, and this time a cataclysmic war, will purge. Their Gallic pride and honor are at stake in this matter, yet, even more, their infamous Gallic greed, for it would be disastrous to their national treasury if upward of $200 million dollars were taken from them . . . especially if it were surrendered to citizens of North America, whom, you know, they scorn as barbarians. The difficulty is, our own government, led by an unholy coalition of Democrats and Republicans, is aiding the French government in its suppression of the case, doubtless because certain high-ranking politicians are accepting 'fees' for their trouble. Already, gentlemen, the Society has been hounded, and threatened, and denounced on the very floor of the Senate, as being *not in the best interests of French-American relations!*" (At which outburst the little audience would exclaim in surprise and perplexity. For things were so much more convoluted than anyone might have thought—!) "Thus, our need to remain entirely underground," Bramhurst said severely, "—pledged to secrecy; indefatigable in our efforts to legitimize the lost Auguste, and his many descendants; and faithful to the death in our willingness to underwrite the lawsuit. For though it *is* proving costly, only think, when it is settled, what rewards will follow: for

Auguste's honor will be restored, after so many years; *and all his living descendants will be wealthy men.*"

The historical facts were: The great Napoléon Bonaparte, exiled on St. Helena after the defeat of Waterloo, sired, in the final year of his life, an illegitimate son with a woman (of noble birth, it was believed, though unrecorded national identity) many years his junior; though the love affair and the subsequent birth were clandestine, the child was eventually baptized in the Catholic faith, as "Emanuel Auguste," sometime in the autumn of 1821; and, as the mother rightfully feared for his life, he was taken away immediately following his father's death,—to reside, in secrecy, in one or another Mediterranean country. (Speculation had it that the Emperor's last *inamorata* was a surpassingly beautiful girl of scarcely sixteen years of age, of richly mixed ancestry,—Spanish, Greek, Moroccan.) In exile, so to speak, the boy grew to his maturity, being aware of his parentage yet resigned to a bastard's fate; until, at the age of twenty-one, he dared venture to Paris, under an assumed name, where he learned that Napoléon had provided for him in his will, and very handsomely too; but that it would be his death to pursue the issue. (For all of France was united by this time under the stern rule of Napoléon III, the late Emperor's nephew.) Being, evidently, a youth of some equanimity, and ill-inclined to greed, Emanuel Auguste resolved to forget his patrimony, and to seek his fortune in Germany (1844–1852), and in England (1852–

59

1879), where he died in a London suburb, known to his neighbors and associates as "E. August Armstrong," a well-respected gentleman in the business of cotton imports. Following his death it became known that, since leaving France, he had taken on a number of pseudonyms, out of necessity,—among then Schneider, Shaffer, Reichard, Paige, Osgood, Brown, and of course Armstrong. Thus, the record of his progeny, and his progeny's progeny was complex indeed—!

For many years following Auguste's death in 1879, he and his mysterious patrimony were forgotten, and his inheritance remained untouched in the vaults of the Bank of Paris. (The original sum was said to be $43 million, in francs; which prodigious sum gradually increased more than tenfold with the passage of years, by way of investments, interest, and the like, under the canny manipulations of the officers of the Bank.) How long the fortune would have remained unclaimed no one could say, were it not for the bold intervention of a gentleman named Heinrich Shaffer, of Manhattan, himself a broker, who, following his discovery of his blood relationship with E. Auguste Napoléon Bonaparte, in 1909, decided to organize the Society. Being fairly wealthy, Shaffer could afford to hire a number of lawyers, historians, and professional genealogists, that the identity of Auguste's descendants might be ascertained throughout the world; and a legal suit initiated against the Bank of Paris, under terms of international law. "It is not for the sake of mere gold that we undertake this campaign," Shaffer said, "—but for the sake of the lost honor of poor Auguste. We, his heirs, his blood descendants, are obliged to claim our rightful patrimony *in his name,*—else we are dishonored indeed."

It was hardly a surprise to the zealous Americans that the Frenchmen who harbored the fortune proved immediately hostile to their efforts; this, indeed, had been expected. (Though Shaffer was gratified to be told, by way of French informants,—"friends," as they called themselves, of the "late wronged heir"—that there had long been a tale of a forsaken inheritance, locked away in the great vaults of the Bank of Paris, and jealously guarded by the highest bank officials, as closely bound up with the sacred memory of the Emperor.) The task of tracing the North American heirs, however, was less onerous than Shaffer had anticipated, for, recognizing the altruistic impulse behind his effort, people were for the most part eager to cooperate.

Thus, by winter of 1912, approximately three hundred heirs had been located in the United States and Canada, and it was estimated that another one hundred, or one hundred fifty, yet remained. (For E. Auguste Napoléon Bonaparte, had, it seems, sired many a child himself, by way of numerous wives and mistresses, under numerous pseudonyms. "It is neither curse nor virtue," Shaffer commented, "—that we Bonapartes are somewhat more lusty than our neighbors!") At the start, Shaffer wanted to restrict the Society to those persons directly descended from Auguste, but, with the passage of time, as more and more parties were taken up with the cause, the membership was relaxed somewhat; though all were of course sworn to absolute secrecy; and all were required to forward dues, legal fees, and various surcharges, payable in cash, by messanger (and not the U.S. Mails) to Shaffer, as President of the Society, or to his authorized agents. (It was carefully explained to the "legitimate" heirs, as, one by one, they were interviewed in the privacy of their homes, that the Society, now five thousand strong, was composed not only of blood relations like themselves, but of parties sworn to pursue Justice,—these being primarily well-to-do gentlemen of the law, religious leaders, historians, etc. who were greatly impressed by Heinrich Shaffer's mission. As the legal struggle lying ahead would demand great sacrifice, these gentlemen were freely donating their time, money, and encouragement, though, when the suit was settled,—in 1915, perhaps, or 1916 at the latest—*they would not receive a penny of the fortune.*)

So far as the Society itself was constituted,—Heinrich Shaffer continued to serve as President, though his health, drained by the activities of the past several years (and not least by various threats against his wellbeing, made by financiers, politicians, and their ilk, in the hire of the French), rarely allowed him to preside over meetings of the Society. (It was rumored too that Shaffer's personal fortune, in excess of $900,000 some years ago, was also being rapidly drained, owing to the costs of underwriting the Society: but this fact Shaffer did not want known to his associates.) Authorized as agents for the Society, for the Mid-Atlantic sector, were Messieurs Gaymead, Lichtman, Bramhurst, and, from time to time, one or two others, all gentlemen with legal and financial training, of the highest personal integrity. It was their task to contact the missing heirs,—to lay out before them, in the privacy of their homes, the various documents (genealogical maps, birth and baptismal certificates, facsimiles of legal records, etc.) pertaining to E. Auguste Napoléon Bonaparte, and to themselves,—to present to them the opportunity of joining the Society, under its necessarily severe terms: absolute secrecy; $2,000 payable within thirty days; and regular dues, fees, surcharges, etc., of various sums (rarely more than $500, depending upon the progress of the lawsuit) from time to time.

Of the numerous heirs who were interviewed by one or another of the Society's agents, nearly all were enthusiastic: for the facts were most convincingly presented; the altruism of Mr. Shaffer and his professional associates was seen to be extraordinary; and the somewhat faint or smudged daguerreotypes of Emanuel Auguste (as a babe-in-arms, as a toddler, as a haughty young gentleman of perhaps twenty-one) never failed to excite special interest. (Indeed, it was remarkable how citizens in such diverse regions of the Mid-Atlantic sector as metropolitan Philadelphia, southeastern New Jersey, and the remote reaches of the upper Delaware Valley, were struck by family resemblances between the lost heir,—as Auguste was frequently called—and themselves or relatives. Again and again young Auguste, though pictured nearly in profile, and with his hooded eyes turned arrogantly away from the camera, was realized as the "living image" of a cousin, an uncle, a grandfather, a father, a child:—and poor patient Mr.

63

Gaymead, no less than his colleagues Lichtman, Bramhurst, Hynd, and Glücklicht, had to endure many a lengthy session, seated on a sofa, being shown a copious family album, with much animated commentary to the effect that the "royal blood" of the Bonapartes had always been evident, though unrecognized as such, in the client's family. It might be a look about the eyes,—or the shape of the nose, the ears, the chin,—the set of the jaw,—the cheekbones, the bones of the forehead, etc.,—but the visual evidence was unmistakable, was it not?)

"Yes, it is so," Mr. Gaymead or one of his colleagues would say, studying a photograph, or the facial bones of a living child presented blushing before him, "—yes, I believe it *is* so. I wonder that your family did not come to the conclusion, some time ago, that you were not quite of common clay, like your neighbors; but clearly possessed of an exceptional history,—and a no less exceptional future."

A curious predicament: that Abraham Licht's passion for any of his business ventures was in precise *disproportion*, as Elisha had long ago learned, to its *success*.

For where plans proceeded smoothly, and clients were persuaded to surrender gratifying sums of money to his pockets, passion quickly waned; and it seemed to the restless entrepreneur that, for all his genius, for all his willingness to risk safety, he must not be playing for high-enough stakes. He frequently confided in Elisha, alone of his children, that difficulties,—challenges,—obstacles,—outright dangers—were what most

64

stirred his spirit, and provided a fit contest for his powers, whose depths (he believed) had not yet been plumbed.

So it happened that "Little Moses" was forced into retirement earlier than seemed absolutely necessary (for Elisha quite delighted in the masquerade, knowing himself, though disguised in the skin of a "darky," *not a Negro at all.*) Similarly, "The Panama Canal, Ltd.," closed its doors to further investors; after so wondrous a six-month showing Abraham Licht halfway feared J. P. Morgan would want to buy him out; likewise "X. X. Anson & Sons Copper, Ltd.," and "North American Liberty Bonds, Inc.," and "Zicht's Etheric Massage" (whereby the afflicted patient, suffering from such ailments as rheumatism, arthritis, migraine, stomach upsets, and mysterious illnesses of all kinds, lay upon a table, in absolute darkness, to be massaged by the "magnetic etheric waves" produced by an "osteophonic" machine of Dr. Zicht's invention); and, not least, the enterprise of the astrological sportsman "A. Washburn Frelicht, Ph.D.," who had triumphed at Chautauqua, and was talked of, still, in racing circles. (It was a measure of Abraham Licht's indifference to past success, or his actual generosity regarding fellow entrepreneurs, that he cared not a whit that tout sheets, or tipster sheets, were now sold openly at American racecourses; and that their indebtedness to the pioneering *Frelicht's Tips* went unacknowledged.)

Of course, not all of Abraham Licht's enterprises were successful; and the comparative, or outright, fail-

65

ures, no less than his half dozen embarrassments with the law, rankled still.

For instance, at the tender age of fifteen he had been ill-used by a kinsman named Nathaniel Liges, of the Onondaga Valley, who had hired him as a lottery-ticket salesman,—and failed to inform him when the news broke, rather suddenly, that the tickets were counterfeit. He had scarcely fared better, when, a few years later, now self-employed, he made the rounds of the Nautauga region as a Bible and patent medicine pedlar,—in the very wake, ironically, of a notorious Dutch pedlar from downstate who offered the same general brand of goods, and resembled young Abraham as a father might resemble a son!

He confided in Elisha one day that, as a brash young man of thirty-two, he had agreed to run for state congress on the Republican ticket in one of the sparsely populated mountain districts north of Muirkirk; but found the campaigning so loathsome an activity, and the prospect of a tame, respectable, *legal* employment so enervating, he soon lost all spirit for the contest, and quite outraged his backers. Moreover, his Democratic opponent was so clearly a self-promoting fool, it seemed an insult to Abraham Licht's dignity to trouble to compete with him. Like Shakespeare's Coriolanus, with whom he closely identified, he felt despoiled by the mere activity of seeking public acclaim in this ignominious way. Here, the Game was of a much lower mettle than he was accustomed to; the prospect of winning over an ignorant electorate excited him as would the prospect of seducing a woman who was both

66

ugly and brain-damaged . . . ! Thus, Abraham soon began to mock his opponent, and the oratorical style of campaigners in general (whether Republican, Democrat, Populist, or other); and finally betrayed his backers by dropping out of the race, and disappearing from the region altogether, a few weeks before the election.

Even so, he told Elisha that he would not rule out the possibility of a political career someday for *him*. "You are worth much more than a mere backcountry congressional seat, of course; your superficial racial component,—or attribute,—or 'talent,' whatever— cannot help but be an asset in the proper circumstances."

Elisha was deeply struck by this remark; yet could not resist assuming a playful tone. "Shall I run for Governor of the state," he asked, "—or, perhaps, for President of the country? Might I be a fit candidate one day for the 'White' House? It would allow my fellow Americans a display of democratic sentiment, to elect a 'darky' to such an office!"

"Don't make light of my proposal," Abraham Licht said severely. "The time is not now; but the time may come. 'Covet where you wish; but never in vain.' "

As with the women Abraham Licht had won, seemingly, and then lost,—his "wives" as he eventually came to call them—so with the business ventures he had never entirely brought to fruition. They haunted; they rankled; they picked and stabbed at his very soul.

Among these was the "E. Auguste Napoléon Bon-

67

aparte" enterprise, first dreamt into being when Abraham Licht was a young man in his twenties; but, owing to limited resources, and exigencies of the moment, never satisfactorily launched. What appealed to Abraham in his maturity was the prospect, regarding the Society, of its *infinite possibility*: once an individual came to believe that royal blood flowed in his veins, and he was a potential heir to a great fortune, how far might his credulity be tested . . . ? No sooner had the Society's roster of "heirs" fulfilled their obligations for one step of the lawsuit (supposedly being fought in a Parisian high court, behind closed doors, by a barrister of international reputation in Mr. Shaffer's employ), than the Society would be forced to assess them yet more: for there was a mare's nest of hidden fees, taxes, "attorneys' retainers," and the like, *with no end in sight*. (Certainly a lawsuit of such complexity would drag on for years and years,—partly as a consequence of French subversion.) In the early spring of '13, a new development arose, forced upon Heinrich Shaffer by several of his associates, who were "gravely concerned" that Shaffer had by this time invested so much of his own money,—nearly $700,000!—while standing to realize, as only *one* heir of Emanuel Auguste, no more money than any other heir; so it was voted by the Society's Board of Governors (in itself a new development, not previously announced to the membership) that members should *invest* in the inheritance itself, rather than merely underwriting the lawsuit. Which is to say, according to the prestigious firm of Robinson & Company, auditors for the Society,—if an

68

individual invests $1 in the inheritance, he will realize $200, when the estate is settled; if an individual invests $1,000, he will realize $200,000; and so forth.

And now, indeed, the race was on . . . !

Abraham Licht was forced to hire a half dozen agents to deal with the heady increase in business. Families mortgaged their houses and property, or sold them with imprudent haste; insurance policies were cashed in; a minister in Penns Neck, New Jersey, borrowed $6,500 from his parishioners with the vague promise of repaying them at 5 percent interest; one member of the Society, by the name of Rheinhardt, secretly took out an insurance policy on his wife for $100,000, with the intention,—as he naively told Mr. Gaymead—of investing the entire sum in Emanuel Auguste "as soon as the old woman dies." (Gaymead had the presence of mind to inform him on the spot that the Board of Governors, just the previous day, had passed a ruling to the effect that no member could invest more than $4,000,—which after all would reap a magnificent $800,000.)

By February of 1913 post office inspectors for several cities suspected that something was afoot, yet, as no one had complained to police, and members of the Society were scrupulous about sending their payments (preferably in cash, though checks were also accepted) to Heinrich Shaffer by way of a messenger service, and never through the U.S. mails, where was the harm . . . ? Members were cautioned repeatedly on this score, for the Postmaster General of the United States was himself in the pay of the French, and prepared to open

69

and destroy any of the Society's correspondence. (So strict was this ruling, members were told that any letter sent by way of the U.S. mails would not be opened; and the sender's membership would be revoked.) For purposes of security, too, the Society's address was frequently changed, being now on Broome Street in lower Manhattan; and now on East Forty-ninth Street; and now on the Upper West Side; then again, rather abruptly, in Teaneck, New Jersey; or in Hudson, New York. In a single week in June 1913 such quantities of money were received, in denominations ranging from $5 to $1,000, that Abraham Licht and Elisha wearied of counting it, giving up after having reached $95,000; —and sweeping it into a burlap sack, to be deposited, under one or another pseudonym (Brisbane, O'Toole, Lichtenstein, Danby) in one or another of the Wall Street investment houses (Knickerbocker Trust, American Savings & Trust, Lynch & Burr, Throckmorton & Co.) Abraham had chosen. He suspected that, by this time, a number of persons in the financial district were watching his activities closely, but in the bliss of triumph he cared not a whit.

He was Abraham Licht, after all,—though not known by that name *here*.

"If, as Jonathan Swift believed, Mankind is to be divided into 'fools' and 'knaves,' " Abraham Licht told Elisha and Millicent, "—is there any greater delight than to be assured of a steady income by the former, as the latter look on in envy?"

Through the long summer of 1913 membership in

70

the Society for the Reclamation and Restoration of E. Auguste Napoléon Bonaparte continued to grow; until, by mid-August, shortly before the entire enterprise had to be abandoned, there were approximately seven thousand members in good standing; and an estimated fortune of $3 million. Both Elisha and Millie were dazed by their father's success, yet apprehensive as well, for were things not going too smoothly? . . . Was there not an air, very nearly palpable at certain times, that they were being scrutinized on every side, yet never approached? Owing to the rapid increase in business, Abraham Licht had had to hire twenty-odd employees,—"solicitors," "agents," "messenger boys," "accountants," "stenographers." These persons, though not in full possession of the facts regarding Emanuel Auguste, were yet experienced enough, and canny enough by instinct, to know that they must not disobey their employer's directives. ("One false step," Abraham Licht cautioned each in turn, "—and the entire house of cards falls. And some of you may deeply regret that it does.")

At this time the Lichts's principal residency was a lavish eight-room suite at the Park Stuyvesant Hotel on Central Park West, though Abraham and Elisha were frequently away overnight on business, and Millie was enrolled as a student in Miss Thayer's Academy for Young Christian Ladies on East Eighty-fifth Street. (Millie did not always attend classes faithfully at Miss Thayer's, being very much caught up in the liveliness of Manhattan, and in the flattering attentions of one or another young gentleman admirer,—whom she

71

might treat with playful coquettish ease, as her heart, in secret, belonged to Elisha.) When all proceeded smoothly, and the Society's demands were not distracting, Abraham Licht liked nothing better than to treat his dear children to a Sunday excursion on the town,—an elegant brunch at the Plaza, a leisurely surrey ride through Central Park, afternoon at the Metropolitan Museum of Art, high tea at the sumptuous Henri IV on Park Avenue, an evening of grand opera (in a single heady season the Lichts heard Wagner, Gluck, Mozart, and the American premiere of Strauss's *Der Rosenkavalier*, during the course of which Abraham Licht fell in love with Anna Case in the role of Sophie), followed by supper at Delmonico's, which might last well beyond midnight.

"How happy we are!—and how simple it is, so suddenly, to be happy!" Millie might whisper, giving Elisha a hasty kiss when they were alone together for a minute or two; and Elisha, who was rather more agitated by love than made happy, and, despite Abraham Licht's success, could not but worry that things might collapse at any hour, found it very difficult to reply. When Millie was gay he believed he ought to be gay in return; yet, when Millie was gay, might she be cleverly testing, to gauge whether such gaiety were appropriate, or no . . . ? It had not been that long a time, by Elisha's private reckoning, since Thurston's death; yet Abraham gave every sign of having succeeded in forgetting him, except for the disconcerting fiction, now and then, expressed to the younger children, that

72

their willful brother was away somewhere, *incommunicado,*—"in Brazil, perhaps, or Patagonia."

("Would it be thus with 'Little Moses,' I wonder, if *I* dared disobey?" Elisha wondered.)

Thus, the careening happiness of these months, which affected Abraham Licht in contradictory ways.

For instance, from time to time he expressed a vague yearning for the country,—for Muirkirk,—which he had not visited in months; but he dared not risk leaving New York until things were, as he put it, more stabilized. He did not altogether trust his hired employees; and, half-whimsical, half-bitter, complained to Elisha and Millie that it would be far easier for him to build a financial empire if he could staff his office with blood relatives. (Had his kin,—the Barracloughs, the Sternlichts, the Ligeses—irrevocably disappointed him?) Then again, perhaps the Society was growing too quickly; perhaps it would be prudent at this point to limit membership; even to introduce a new development . . . things being so hopelessly snarled in Paris, and the French courts so mired in corruption, a mistrial had been called; and an entirely new case would have to be prepared, for presentation in, say, January 1914 . . . ? This had its appeal, and met with approval (and no little relief) on the part of Elisha; for by now Abraham Licht was several times a millionaire, as O'Toole, Brisbane, Lichtenstein, and Danby, and could surely afford to relax; for his fortune was in safe hands in the very best Wall Street investment houses; and would eventually double, or triple, or, this being America, quadruple . . . would it not?

73

And Abraham Licht, for all his vigor and optimism, was not quite so young as he had been, even a few years before.

Then, abruptly, after an irritable breakfast of skimming through the New York newspapers, and reading, for instance, of the wedding of Miss Vivien Gould, granddaughter of the infamous Gould, to Lord Decies of His Majesty's Seventh Hussars, at Saint Bartholomew's Chuch close by, how could he rest content with the meager millions *he* had earned: was it not preposterous for him to imagine himself wealthy, set beside such persons? (The Goulds were so inestimably rich, their empire so totally beyond calculation, it was noted without comment in the tabloid papers that 225 seamstresses had labored on the bride's trousseau; the cake alone cost $1,000,—with its electric lights and tiny sugar cupids bearing the Decies coat of arms; the bride's father presented her with a diamond coronet worth $1 million; and other gifts, given by such members of the international social set as Pierpont Morgan, Lord and Lady Ashburton, Mrs. Stuyvesant Fish, the Duke of Connaught, Mrs. Astor, Mrs. Vanderbilt, et al., were of like value.) "No, I am hardly wealthy," Abraham Licht mused, not caring whether Millie, or Elisha, or a servant overheard, "—I hardly *exist*, in truth. And what shall I do about it, at the age of fifty-two?"

So that day, and for several days following, he might well be caught up in one of his fevers of planning: he would hire yet more employees, wooing them away, perhaps, from their Wall Street firms; he would begin

74

a fresh campaign into Virginia, North Carolina, South Carolina, Georgia, where blood descendants of Emanuel Auguste doubtless existed, awaiting discovery ("the farther south, the greater the fools"); he would summon New York City's most prestigious architect to discuss the Italianate villa he wanted built,—on the corner of Park Avenue and East Sixty-sixth, perhaps, but a stone's throw from the Vanderbilt mansion. And one day, even, if all proceeded smoothly, one day *soon*, Abraham Licht would march as proudly up Saint Bartholomew's as had Mr. George Gould, with a far lovelier daughter on his arm, to be given away, in Holy Matrimony, to a Lord, or a Count, or a Duke,—if not a Prince.

By the end of the summer, however, Abraham was forced to the conclusion that the Society for the Reclamation and Restoration of E. Auguste Napoléon Bonaparte had become rather too successful and would have to be curtailed soon, or abandoned altogether. (For one thing, Abraham surely could *not* trust his employees, some of whom were extremely clever young men. For another, he had begun to discover perplexing news items in the papers, having to do with rumors of an "international scandal" involving, variously, an illegitimate son of a Hapsburg duke, an illegitimate daughter of the late King Edward VII, several great-grandchildren of Napoléon Bonaparte, and, most tantalizing to inhabitants of New York State, a direct descendant of the Dauphin, King Louis

75

XVII, who had, according to legend, escaped France, and hidden himself away in the general area of the Chautauqua Mountains, north of Mt. Chattaroy.)

Consequently, a special meeting of the Society's shareholders was held in the Sixth Regiment Armory, in northeastern Philadelphia, immediately after Labor Day. Several thousand heirs of Emanuel Auguste crowded into the building, after having identified themselves at the closely guarded doors, and paying an admission fee of $2, to help underwrite the considerable cost of renting the armory. (In truth, the armory was made available to the Society for a token $100, by way of a Philadelphia gentleman named Browne, who had invested a full $4,000 in the inheritance.) The atmosphere was expectant and rather highly charged, since the members had been alerted that they would at last be introduced to their President, Heinrich Shaffer; would be informed of the latest "and somewhat disturbing" news regarding the lawsuit in Paris; and would be presented, as a bonus, with *a full-blooded descendant of Emanuel Auguste*, arrived in the States only the previous week.

The armory was a plain, utilitarian space, made cleverly attractive by numerous strategically placed posters of Emanuel Auguste, as a babe-in-arms, as a toddler, and as a handsome young rake,—familiar likenesses, of course, though the enlargement process had mysteriously coarsened and darkened the image. On stage, beside the lectern, were an American flag and a peacock-blue flag bearing the royal coat of arms of the Bonaparte family, or a reasonable facsimile thereof;

placed about the stage were floral displays of ingeniously natural-looking wax calla lilies, white carnations, and white irises, donated by a funeral director named Osgood, of suburban Philadelphia. The crowd, 5,800 strong, consisted primarily of men, with a sprinkling of women, and gave off an air of goodwill charged with apprehension. For all beneath this roof were blood relations, however widely separated by accidents of birth,—yet, each having invested in the Bonaparte fortune, was he not, in a sense, a rival to the others? Could he, indeed, *trust* the others?

Reasoning that the audience would be grateful for a familiar face, Abraham Licht began the meeting in the guise of the brisk, punctilious, yet altogether comforting Bramhurst, who wore a new suit in honor of the occasion, and sported a pale-pink carnation in his buttonhole; and proved, to everyone's delight, a superlative public speaker. In a ringing voice he commanded that the doors to the armory be locked, as it was 8:06 P.M., and no more latecomers would be tolerated. (Which severe measure was met with a wave of satisfaction on the part of the nervous heirs, some of whom had been waiting since midafternoon for the doors to be opened.) Next, Bramhurst spoke forcefully of the Society's history,—its ideals,—its fidelity to Emanuel Auguste,—the loyalty, generosity, and collective moral courage of its members, etc.; he concluded by promising that no one in the hall would leave this evening without "a heartwarming vision indelibly engraved on his soul." Then, he introduced a Mr. Banting, tall, full-chested, smiling, the chairman of the Board of

77

Governors, who in turn spoke heartily of the Society's aims, and in particular of Heinrich Shaffer's energy, charity, selflessness, imagination, guidance, etc. (This gentleman, a hireling of Abraham Licht's, was an intriguing character in himself,—an occasional accountant, chorus boy, racetrack tout, and artiste.)

Greeted by near-ecstatic applause, frowning just perceptively, and walking with a cane, was the esteemed President Heinrich Shaffer,—upon whom all eyes avidly fixed. An aristocratic figure, certainly; frail with age; white-haired; impeccably dressed in a dark pin-striped suit and gray silk vest, with a white handkerchief tucked into his pocket; with slightly hollowed cheeks, a narrow chin, a wattled neck; tinted spectacles; and, most curious, a skin so darkly tanned, one might almost have imagined him of foreign extraction. . . . Yet all doubts were assuaged once the applause died away and Shaffer began to speak, for it was clear immediately, by his accent, that he could be no other than American; and Caucasian.

Shaffer differed significantly from the speakers who preceded him, by wasting no time in winning over his audience; for, as he said, there was urgent business at hand; and "time and tide wait for no man." He began by telling the membership that they were not only united in a common cause for justice, they were all blood relations, if only to an infinitesimal degree; and that they were obliged to trust one another as they trusted their solicitor, or their President himself,— albeit there were rumors of informants in their midst, in the pay of the government of France. ("Yet these are but rumors," Shaffer said with an ironical ring to his voice, "—and not entirely to be credited.") Next, the white-haired gentleman spent several minutes assailing those members of the Society ("some of whom are seated in this very hall") who were behind on their dues, yet confident, this being America, after all, and not France, that their comrades would compensate for their dereliction of duty. Poking the air with a long forefinger, Shaffer chided such slothful descendants of the tragic Emanuel Auguste; and went on to criticize, as well, those who had attempted to bribe Messieurs Gaymead, Lichtman, Bramhurst, Glücklicht, et al., into allowing them, under assumed names, to invest more than $4,000 in the inheritance. ("For what do you think would follow, gentlemen, if certain of your greedy comrades invested $40,000,—$400,000,—$1 million in Emanuel Auguste's money?" Shaffer demanded, his voice trembling in elderly contempt. He paused dramatically, leaning over the podium, and staring out into the sea of frightened faces. "I will tell you, gentlemen: *there would not be enough money for the honest investors, when the lawsuit is settled.*")

At which point a panicked hush fell over the gathering.

However, Shaffer said, no officer of the Society would stoop to bribe-taking; so there was no danger in *that* quarter.

Next, Shaffer read a cable from his Parisian barrister,

79

received only a few days before, to the effect that the meticulously constructed case for the claimants had been undercut by subversive elements, doubtless from within; that the highest judge of the highest court in the land had confided in him, in private, that it would be in the best interests of the Society for the present suit to be dropped, and a new suit initiated after 1 January 1914, to ensure a court "free and clear of jurist prejudice." These words were read in a quavering voice, that revealed how deeply moved Heinrich Shaffer was by this development, despite his brusque tone. (Indeed, there was a fearful pause, during which the old man seemed about to burst into tears; and fumbled to draw his handkerchief from his pocket.) Very quickly, however, he recovered,—told the gathering in a voice heavy with irony that such news would delight the *saboteurs* in their midst, yet would not, he swore, be a source of despair to *him*, though, at his age, it was no longer altogether reasonable to expect that he might live to see Emanuel Auguste restored to his lost honor.

Yet, having waited so long, no one would object, he supposed, to waiting a few months longer: for Rome, after all, "was not built in a day."

At which dramatic point a scattering of individuals in the hall broke into applause; and, within fifteen seconds, were joined by the remainder of the enormous crowd,—so that wave upon wave of generous clapping filled the armory, and cheers, whistles, and shouts of Bravo!—bringing tears to a proud old man's eyes.

It was all Shaffer could do to quiet the crowd, after

this interruption of two or three minutes, and continue with his remarks.

He thanked them humbly for their vote of confidence; reiterated his statement that a six-month delay in the lawsuit would not be a source of despair to *him*; calculated that the suit would "very likely" be settled by the end of 1916, at the latest; and that, with interest being compounded daily,—indeed, hourly—the fortune would by that time be worth nearly $300,000,000, according to the most recent estimate of the conservative New York accounting firm Hearns, Saddler.

At which point more applause ensued, as tumultuous as before.

The surprise of the evening immediately followed, being, as Heinrich Shaffer said, the only pure-blooded living descendant of Emanuel Auguste Napoléon Bonaparte,—a native-born Moroccan, by the name of François Joliet Mazare Napoléon Bonaparte, twenty-five years of age, and freshly arrived on these shores. Would the membership be gracious enough, please, to welcome their privileged visitor—?

Thus, applause began; and numerous persons at the rear and extreme sides of the hall rose to their feet, to get a clearer view; but, ah! what consternation, when, in a crimson velvet suit with knee breeches, and a plumed hat, and wearing a gilded dress sword, *a young Negro appeared!*—as assured, insouciant, and feckless, as if he were not only of the white race, but of royal blood indeed.

At which point another panicked hush fell over the hall. Those who had risen from their seats stood paralyzed, staring.

Negro...?

Taking no notice of his audience, Heinrich Shaffer proudly drew the young man forward and introduced him: Monsieur François Joliet Mazare Napoléon Bonaparte, the purest-blooded of all Emanuel Auguste's descendants. He embraced François with great warmth; and, as if such behavior were commonplace to these shores, kissed him resoundingly on both cheeks—! The handsome Negro's eyes and teeth flashed white; his skin gleamed and winked, as if oiled; in an extravagant gesture he whipped his plumed hat from his head, and bowed low before his silent audience.

Still taking no notice of the unnatural quiet in the hall, Shaffer stood with his arm draped paternally across François's shoulders, and spoke at length, and with some passion, of the fact that, according to the most meticulous genealogical charts, *here* stood the embodiment of Emanuel Auguste himself; that the lost heir's pedigreed blood beat fiercely and proudly in François's veins, as, to a less concentrated degree, it did in theirs; that young François deserved no less than a princedom in France, once the estate was settled.

Negro...?

As the dashing young man could speak no English, his speech to the crowd was unintelligible, though rapid, charming, and seemingly assured. He interrupted his own cascade of words with brief asides, doubtless witty; he laughed; he showed wide white

82

childish teeth; his hand gestures were flamboyant. He had nothing of the cautious, craven air of an American black, for it was clear that he *was* of princely blood, and might be excused for thinking so highly of himself. Yet his audience sat speechless,—paralyzed. Here and there one might have seen a face lightly touched with repugnance, or even revulsion; some were frankly perplexed; others looked from François to the posters of his noble ancestor, and back again, and took note too of the deeply tanned Heinrich Shaffer whose skin contrasted so strangely with his white hair and his impeccably "white" manner; what did such things mean?

So swiftly did the young Negro jabber in his exotic native tongue, even those who knew a word or two of French could not have hoped to grasp his meaning: "*Je hais! tu hais! il hais! nous haissons! vous haissez! ils haissent! pied! kangourou! merde! merde blanc! merde noire! merde pure! merde purée!*—"

Shortly thereafter, not long past 8:30 P.M., the meeting came to an end.

Mr. Banting, flushed and smiling, graciously reappeared at the lectern, to reiterate the "high points" of the session: the temporary suspension of the lawsuit in the Court of Paris; the temporary suspension of all investments, until further notice; the need to maintain faith in the Society,—and to keep the vow of absolute secrecy.

By this time, however, very few parties were listening. Many had already risen from their seats, somber, abashed, stricken, eager, it seemed, to get away quickly, without lingering to applaud Mr. Banting; and without wishing to look too closely at their neighbors.

Afterward, a triumphant Abraham Licht proposed a champagne toast to Elisha; told him that he had performed beautifully,—irresistibly; as delightful as anything in *opéra bouffe* (including the aria); and deserving of far more applause than the fools had granted him. For, like any consummate player of the Game, he knew his audience; he plumbed the depths of their souls.

But Elisha, oddly, did not fall in with the celebratory mood. His reply was a cold vague murmur, subtly ironic.

"Yes Father thank you Father *yes* Father,—I know them well."

Chee's Witch

TONY HILLERMAN

Tony Hillerman has written six mystery novels steeped in the culture of the Navajo and Pueblo Indians. He won an Edgar for Dance Hall of the Dead *(1973). About "Chee's Witch," Mr. Hillerman notes: "In this short story I was seeing if something could be done with two ideas: first, I wanted to use the Navajo belief that witches use the skin that has the 'wind marks' on the fingertips, palms, et cetera, to make 'corpse powder' and handle it as a way to avoid identification of body; second, I wanted to try the notion of switching a protected witness under the noses of the federals. Readers of my books may notice that one of these ideas later became an important part of* The Dark Wind *and the other the key to* The Ghostway."

SNOW IS SO IMPORTANT to the Eskimos they have nine nouns to describe its variations. Corporal Jimmy Chee of the Navajo Tribal Police had heard that as an anthropology student at the University of New Mexico. He remembered it now because he was thinking of all the words you need in Navajo to account for the many forms of witchcraft. The word Old Woman Tso had used was "anti'l," which is the ultimate sort, the absolute worst. And so, in fact, was the deed which seemed to have been done. Murder, apparently. Mutilation, certainly, if Old Woman Tso had her facts right. And then, if one believed all the mythology of witchery told among the fifty clans who comprised The People, there must also be cannibalism, incest, even necrophilia.

On the radio in Chee's pickup truck, the voice of the young Navajo reading a Gallup used-car commercial was replaced by Willie Nelson singing of trouble and a worried mind. The ballad fit Chee's mood. He was tired. He was thirsty. He was sticky with sweat. He was worried. His pickup jolted along the ruts in a windless heat, leaving a white fog of dust to mark its winding passage across the Rainbow Plateau. The truck was gray with it. So was Jimmy Chee. Since sunrise he had covered maybe two hundred miles of half-graded gravel and unmarked wagon tracks of the Arizona–Utah–New Mexico border country. Routine at first—a check into a witch story at the Tsossie hogan north of Teec Nos Pos to stop trouble before it started. Routine and logical. A bitter winter, a sand stormspring, a summer of rainless, desiccating heat. Hopes dying, things going wrong, anger growing, and then the witch gossip. The logical. A bitter winter, a sand storm spring, a summer awry. The trouble at the summer hogan of the Tsossies was a sick child and a water well that had turned alkaline—nothing unexpected. But you didn't expect such a specific witch. The skinwalker, the Tsossies agreed, was The City Navajo, the man who had come to live in one of the government houses at Kayenta.

86

Why the City Navajo? Because everybody knew he was a witch. Where had they heard that, the first time? The People who came to the trading post at Mexican Water said it. And so Chee had driven westward over Tohache Wash, past Red Mesa and Rabbit Ears to Mexican Water. He had spent hours on the shady porch giving those who came to buy, and to fill their water barrels, and to visit, a chance to know who he was until finally they might risk talking about witchcraft to a stranger. They were Mud Clan, and Many Goats People, and Standing Rock Clan—foreign to Chee's own Slow Talking People—but finally some of them talked a little.

A witch was at work on the Rainbow Plateau. Adeline Etcitty's mare had foaled a two-headed colt. Hosteen Musket had seen the witch. He'd seen a man walk into a grove of cottonwoods, but when he got there an owl flew away. Rudolph Bisti's boys lost three rams while driving their flocks up into the Chuska high pastures, and when they found the bodies, the huge tracks of a werewolf were all around them. The daughter of Rosemary Nashibitti had seen a big dog bothering her horses and had shot at it with her .22 and the dog had turned into a man wearing a wolfskin and had fled, half running, half flying. The old man they called Afraid of His Horses had heard the sound of the witch on the roof of his winter hogan, and saw the dirt falling through the smoke hole as the skinwalker tried to throw in his corpse powder. The next morning the old man had followed the tracks of the Navajo Wolf for a mile, hoping to kill him. But the tracks had faded

87

away. There was nothing very unusual in the stories, except their number and the recurring hints that City Navajo was the witch. But then came what Chee hadn't expected. The witch had killed a man.

The police dispatcher at Window Rock had been interrupting Willie Nelson with an occasional blurted message. Now she spoke directly to Chee. He acknowledged. She asked his location.

"About fifteen miles south of Dennehotso," Chee said. "Homeward bound for Tuba City. Dirty, thirsty, hungry, and tired."

"I have a message."

"Tuba City," Chee repeated, "which I hope to reach in about two hours, just in time to avoid running up a lot of overtime for which I never get paid."

"The message is FBI Agent Wells needs to contact you. Can you make a meeting at Kayenta Holiday Inn at eight P.M.?"

"What's it about?" Chee asked. The dispatcher's name was Virgie Endecheenie, and she had a very pretty voice and the first time Chee had met her at the Window Rock headquarters of the Navajo Tribal Police he had been instantly smitten. Unfortunately, Virgie was a born-into Salt Cedar Clan, which was the clan of Chee's father, which put an instant end to that. Even thinking about it would violate the complex incest taboo of the Navajos.

"Nothing on what it's about," Virgie said, her voice strictly business. "It just says confirm meeting time and place with Chee or obtain alternate time."

88

"Any first name on Wells?" Chee asked. The only FBI Wells he knew was Jake Wells. He hoped it wouldn't be Jake.

"Negative on the first name," Virgie said.

"All right," Chee said. "I'll be there."

The road tilted downward now into the vast barrens of erosion which the Navajos call Beautiful Valley. Far to the west, the edge of the sun dipped behind a cloud—one of the line of thunderheads forming in the evening heat over the San Francisco Peaks and the Coconino Rim. The Hopis had been holding their Niman Kachina dances, calling the clouds to come and bless them.

Chee reached Kayenta just a little late. It was early twilight and the clouds had risen black against the sunset. The breeze brought the faint smells that rising humidity carry across desert country—the perfume of sage, creosote brush, and dust. The desk clerk said that Wells was in room 284 and the first name was Jake. Chee no longer cared. Jake Wells was abrasive but he was also smart. He had the best record in the special FBI Academy class Chee had attended, a quick, tough intelligence. Chee could tolerate the man's personality for a while to learn what Wells could make of his witchcraft puzzle.

"It's unlocked," Wells said. "Come on in." He was propped against the padded headboard of the bed, shirt off, shoes on, glass in hand. He glanced at Chee and then back at the television set. He was as tall as Chee remembered, and the eyes were just as blue. He

89

waved the glass at Chee without looking away from the set. "Mix yourself one," he said, nodding toward a bottle beside the sink in the dressing alcove.

"How you doing, Jake?" Chee asked.

Now the blue eyes reexamined Chee. The question in them abruptly went away. "Yeah," Wells said. "You were the one at the Academy." He eased himself on his left elbow and extended a hand. "Jake Wells," he said.

Chee shook the hand. "Chee," he said.

Wells shifted his weight again and handed Chee his glass. "Pour me a little more while you're at it," he said, "and turn down the sound."

Chee turned down the sound.

"About 30 percent booze," Wells demonstrated the proportion with his hands. "This is your district then. You're in charge around Kayenta? Window Rock said I should talk to you. They said you were out chasing around in the desert today. What are you working on?"

"Nothing much," Chee said. He ran a glass of water, drinking it thirstily. His face in the mirror was dirty— the lines around mouth and eyes whitish with dust. The sticker on the glass reminded guests that the laws of the Navajo Tribal Council prohibited possession of alcoholic beverages on the reservation. He refilled his own glass with water and mixed Wells's drink. "As a matter of fact, I'm working on a witchcraft case."

"Witchcraft?" Wells laughed. "Really?" He took the drink from Chee and examined it. "How does it work? Spells and like that?"

"Not exactly," Chee said. "It depends. A few years

ago a little girl got sick down near Burnt Water. Her dad killed three people with a shotgun. He said they blew corpse powder on his daughter and made her sick."

Wells was watching him. "The kind of crime where you have the insanity plea."

"Sometimes," Chee said. "Whatever you have, witch talk makes you nervous. It happens more when you have a bad year like this. You hear it and you try to find out what's starting it before things get worse."

"So you're not really expecting to find a witch?"

"Usually not," Chee said.

"Usually?"

"Judge for yourself," Chee said. "I'll tell you what I've picked up today. You tell me what to make of it. Have time?"

Wells shrugged. "What I really want to talk about is a guy named Simon Begay." He looked quizzically at Chee. "You heard the name?"

"Yes," Chee said.

"Well, shit," Wells said. "You shouldn't have. What do you know about him?"

"Showed up maybe three months ago. Moved into one of those U.S. Public Health Service houses over by the Kayenta clinic. Stranger. Keeps to himself. From off the reservation somewhere. I figured you federals put him here to keep him out of sight."

Wells frowned. "How long you known about him?"

"Quite a while," Chee said. He'd known about Begay within a week after his arrival.

"He's a witness," Wells said. "They broke a car-

91

theft operation in Los Angeles. Big deal. National connections. One of those where they have hired hands picking up expensive models and they drive 'em right on the ship and off-load in South America. This Begay is one of the hired hands. Nobody much. Criminal record going all the way back to juvenile, but all nickel-and-dime stuff. I gather he saw some things that help tie some big boys into the crime, so Justice made a deal with him."

"And they hide him out here until the trial?"

Something apparently showed in the tone of the question. "If you want to hide an apple, you drop it in with the other apples," Wells said. "What better place?"

Chee had been looking at Wells's shoes, which were glossy with polish. Now he examined his own boots, which were not. But he was thinking of Justice Department stupidity. The appearance of any new human in a country as empty as the Navajo Reservation provoked instant interest. If the stranger was a Navajo, there were instant questions. What was his clan? Who was his mother? What was his father's clan? Who were his relatives? The City Navajo had no answers to any of these crucial questions. He was (as Chee had been repeatedly told) unfriendly. It was quickly guessed that he was a "relocation Navajo," born to one of those hundreds of Navajo families which the federal government had tried to reestablish forty years ago in Chicago, Los Angeles, and other urban centers. He was a stranger. In a year of witches, he would certainly be suspected. Chee sat looking at his boots, wondering if that was the only basis for the charge that City Navajo was a skinwalker. Or had someone seen something? Had someone seen the murder?

"The thing about apples is they don't gossip," Chee said.

"You hear gossip about Begay?" Wells was sitting up now, his feet on the floor.

"Sure," Chee said. "I hear he's a witch."

Wells produced a pro-forma chuckle. "Tell me about it," he said.

Chee knew exactly how he wanted to tell it. Wells would have to wait a while before he came to the part about Begay. "The Eskimos have nine nouns for snow," Chee began. He told Wells about the variety of witchcraft on the reservations and its environs: about frenzy witchcraft, used for sexual conquests, of witchery distortions, of curing ceremonials, of the exotic two-heart witchcraft of the Hopi Fog Clan, of the Zuni Sorcery Fraternity, of the Navajo "chindi," which is more like a ghost than a witch, and finally of the Navajo Wolf, the anti'l witchcraft, the werewolves who pervert every taboo of the Navajo Way and use corpse powder to kill their victims.

Wells rattled the ice in his glass and glanced at his watch.

"To get to the part about your Begay," Chee said, "about two months ago we started picking up witch gossip. Nothing much, and you expect it during a drought. Lately it got to be more than usual." He described some of the tales and how uneasiness and dread had spread across the plateau. He described what he

93

had learned today, the Tsossies's naming City Navajo as the witch, his trip to Mexican Water, of learning there that the witch had killed a man.

"They said it happened in the spring—couple of months ago. They told me the ones who knew about it were the Tso outfit." The talk of murder, Chee noticed, had revived Wells's interest. "I went up there," he continued, "and found the old woman who runs the outfit. Emma Tso. She told me her son-in-law had been out looking for some sheep, and smelled something, and found the body under some chamiso brush in a dry wash. A witch had killed him."

"How—"

Chee cut off the question. "I asked her how he knew it was a witch killing. She said the hands were stretched out like this." Chee extended his hands, palms up. "They were flayed. The skin was cut off the palms and fingers."

Wells raised his eyebrows.

"That's what the witch uses to make corpse powder," Chee explained. "They take the skin that has the whorls and ridges of the individual personality—the skin from the palms and the finger pads, and the soles of the feet. They take that, and the skin from the glans of the penis, and the small bones where the neck joins the skull, and they dry it, and pulverize it, and use it as poison."

"You're going to get to Begay any minute now," Wells said. "That right?"

"We got to him," Chee said. "He's the one they think is the witch. He's the City Navajo."

94

"I thought you were going to say that," Wells said. He rubbed the back of his hand across one blue eye. "City Navajo. Is it that obvious?"

"Yes," Chee said. "And then he's a stranger. People suspect strangers."

"Were they coming around him? Accusing him? Any threats? Anything like that, you think?"

"It wouldn't work that way—not unless somebody had someone in their family killed. The way you deal with a witch is hire a singer and hold a special kind of curing ceremony. That turns the witchcraft around and kills the witch."

Wells made an impatient gesture. "Whatever," he said. "I think something has made this Begay spooky." He stared into his glass, communing with the bourbon. "I don't know."

"Something unusual about the way he's acting?"

"Hell of it is I don't know how he usually acts. This wasn't my case. The agent who worked him retired or some damn thing, so I got stuck with being the delivery man." He shifted his eyes from glass to Chee. "But if it was me, and I was holed up here waiting, and the guy came along who was going to take me home again, then I'd be glad to see him. Happy to have it over with. All that."

"He wasn't?"

Wells shook his head. "Seemed edgy. Maybe that's natural, though. He's going to make trouble for some hard people."

"I'd be nervous," Chee said.

"I guess it doesn't matter much anyway," Wells

95

said. "He's small potatoes. The guy who's handling it now in the U.S. Attorney's Office said it must have been a toss-up whether to fool with him at all. He said the assistant who handled it decided to hide him out just to be on the safe side."

"Begay doesn't know much?"

"I guess not. That, and they've got better witnesses."

"So why worry?"

Wells laughed. "I bring this sucker back and they put him on the witness stand and he answers all the questions with I don't know and it makes the USDA look like a horse's ass. When a U.S. Attorney looks like that, he finds an FBI agent to blame it on." He yawned. "Therefore," he said through the yawn, "I want to ask you what you think. This is your territory. You are the officer in charge. Is it your opinion that someone got to my witness?"

Chee let the question hang. He spent a fraction of a second reaching the answer, which was they could have if they wanted to try. Then he thought about the real reason Wells had kept him working late without a meal or a shower. Two sentences in Wells's report. One would note that the possibility the witness had been approached had been checked with local Navajo Police. The next would report whatever Chee said next. Wells would have followed Federal Rule One—Protect Your Ass.

Chee shrugged. "You want to hear the rest of my witchcraft business?"

Wells put his drink on the lamp table and untied his shoe. "Does it bear on this?"

96

"Who knows? Anyway there's not much left. I'll let you decide. The point is we had already picked up this corpse Emma Tso's son-in-law found. Somebody had reported it weeks ago. It had been collected, and taken in for an autopsy. The word we got on the body was Navajo male in his thirties probably. No identification on him."

"How was this bird killed?"

"No sign of foul play," Chee said. "By the time the body was brought in, decay and the scavengers hadn't left a lot. Mostly bone and gristle, I guess. This was a long time after Emma Tso's son-in-law saw him."

"So why do they think Begay killed him?" Wells removed his second shoe and headed for the bathroom.

Chee picked up the telephone and dialed the Kayenta clinic. He got the night supervisor and waited while the supervisor dug out the file. Wells came out of the bathroom with his toothbrush. Chee covered the mouthpiece. "I'm having them read me the autopsy report," Chee explained. Wilson began brushing his teeth at the sink in the dressing alcove. The voice of the night supervisor droned into Chee's ear.

"That all?" Chee asked. "Nothing added on? No identity yet? Still no cause?"

"That's him," the voice said.

"How about shoes?" Chee asked. "He have shoes on?"

"Just a sec," the voice said. "Yep. Size 10D. And a hat, and . . ."

"No mention of the neck or skull, right? I didn't miss that? No bones missing?"

97

Silence. "Nothing about neck or skull bones."

"Ah," Chee said. "Fine. I thank you." He felt great. He felt wonderful. Finally things had clicked into place. The witch was exorcised. "Jake," he said. "Let me tell you a little more about my witch case."

Wells was rinsing his mouth. He spit out the water and looked at Chee, amused. "I didn't think of this before," Wells said, "but you really don't have a witch problem. If you leave that corpse a death by natural causes, there's no case to work. If you decide it's a homicide, you don't have jurisdiction anyway. Homicide on an Indian reservation, FBI has jurisdiction." Wells grinned. "We'll come in and find your witch for you."

Chee looked at his boots, which were still dusty. His appetite had left him, as it usually did an hour or so after he missed a meal. He still hungered for a bath. He picked up his hat and pushed himself to his feet.

"I'll go home now," he said. "The only thing you don't know about the witch case is what I just got from the autopsy report. The corpse had his shoes on and no bones were missing from the base of the skull."

Chee opened the door and stood in it, looking back. Wells was taking his pajamas out of his suitcase. "So what advice do you have for me? What can you tell me about my witch case?"

"To tell the absolute truth, Chee, I'm not into witches," Wells said. "Haven't been since I was a boy."

"But we don't really have a witch case now," Chee said. He spoke earnestly. "The shoes were still on, so the skin wasn't taken from the soles of his feet. No

98

bones missing from the neck. You need those to make corpse powder."

Wells was pulling his undershirt over his head. Chee hurried.

"What we have now is another little puzzle," Chee said. "If you're not collecting stuff for corpse powder, why cut the skin off this guy's hands?"

"I'm going to take a shower," Wells said. "Got to get my Begay back to LA tomorrow."

Outside the temperature had dropped. The air moved softly from the west, carrying the smell of rain. Over the Utah border, over the Cococino Rim, over the Rainbow Plateau, lightning flickered and glowed. The storm had formed. The storm was moving. The sky was black with it. Chee stood in the darkness, listening to the mutter of thunder, inhaling the perfume, exulting in it.

He climbed into the truck and started it. How had they set it up, and why? Perhaps the FBI agent who knew Begay had been ready to retire. Perhaps an accident had been arranged. Getting rid of the assistant prosecutor who knew the witness would have been even simpler—a matter of hiring him away from the government job. That left no one who knew this minor witness was not Simon Begay. And who was he? Probably they had other Navajos from the Los Angeles community stealing cars for them. Perhaps that's what had suggested the scheme. To most white men all Navajos looked pretty much alike, just as in his first years at college all Chee had seen in white men was pink skin, freckles, and light-colored eyes. And what would the impostor say? Chee grinned. He'd say whatever was necessary to cast doubt on the prosecution, to cast the fatal "reasonable doubt," to make—as Wells had put it—the U.S. District Attorney look like a horse's ass.

Chee drove into the rain twenty miles west of Kayenta. Huge, cold drops drummed on the pickup roof and turned the highway into a ribbon of water. Tomorrow the backcountry roads would be impassable. As soon as they dried and the washouts had been repaired, he'd go back to the Tsossie hogan, and the Tso place, and to all the other places from which the word would quickly spread. He'd tell the people that the witch was in custody of the FBI and was gone forever from the Rainbow Plateau.

The Blue Book of Crime

JEROME CHARYN

Jerome Charyn has written eighteen novels since 1964—including the Isaac Sidel police tetralogy: Blue Eyes, Marilyn the Wild, The Education of Patrick Silver, *and* Secret Isaac. *William Plummer, writing in the* New York Times Book Review, *has identified him as "one of our most consistently daring and interesting writers." Mr. Charyn's fiction is distinguished by its innovative narrative techniques and probing wit—which are evident here. "The Blue Book of Crime" is the first of a series of interlocking stories in progress.*

DIDN'T LEARN our thieving at the movies. We watched Lawrence Tierney play Dillinger at the RKO, but Talbot and I weren't really Dillinger people. We had our own ideas about crime, and we happened to like Tierney's looks. Nineteen forty-six was the year of Lawrence Tierney. His picture invaded all the movie magazines. He was seen with Carole Landis two years before she killed herself. He was seen with Esther Williams and Diana Lynn. There was talk of Tierney playing young Stalin for Cecil B. De Mille, but De Mille must have changed his mind.

There wasn't much Technicolor in 1946, and it was difficult to speak of Tierney's eyes. Were they blue like Talbot's, or brown like mine? Whatever the truth of his eyes, the neighborhood called me young Dillinger. And Talbot was young Dillinger's friend.

We had a smart cover in Tierney, because no one ever thought of us as thieves. Talbot was the spelling champion at school. He'd started *War and Peace*. His vocabulary was stupendous for someone in the sixth grade. But vocabulary lists didn't lead us to crime. We observed the terrain, saw shops fat with merchandise we admired. We weren't venal. Talbot wouldn't have considered making a profit from the Tommy Henrich glove he stole from Sheridan's store. Our families might have bought us gloves if we had cried long enough, but crying wasn't a strategy we believed in.

Talbot's dad was a taxi driver. My dad sold paper bags, but he'd removed himself from circulation. He wouldn't go out and sell. He suffered from melancholy. He'd become an air-raid warden in 1943 and he lost interest in paper bags the moment he donned his warden's white hat.

He fell into ruin at the end of the war when he had to return the white hat. He sold his paper-bag route to a younger salesman and sat in bed like a man who'd been demobilized and couldn't adjust to civilian life.

The first act of Young Dillinger & Co. involved a pair of bedroom slippers for Dad. We crawled through a duct in back of Sheridan's department store at half-past eight and were out by a quarter to nine. We never took more than one or two items on a particular crawl. That way Sheridan couldn't have discovered the slippage at his store.

I invented phantom jobs for Talbot and me to explain our sudden wealth of merchandise. We still had to sock most of the stuff into an old storage trunk in the basement of Talbot's apartment building. We didn't have to worry about thieves in the building. Neighbors wouldn't have interfered with a trunk that was never locked. Talbot's genius told him that.

His one bit of caution was to read *The Blue Book of Crime*, a primer put out by the FBI. *The Blue Book* wasn't moralistic. It mentioned Dillinger's demise at the hand of FBI agents, but *The Blue Book* wouldn't gloat. "Perhaps we shall never understand the criminal mind. It's as variable as the seven seas. It makes its home among the poor, the middling, and the very rich. It has no occupational boundary. It can be perverse, dull, or mathematically precise. If we forget this, criminal justice shall always remain a bumbling stepchild to crime."

That stepchild appeared to us in the form of Bob, a Bronx policeman who was in love with Talbot's big sister, Girlie. Bob seemed gentle for a cop. He was six-two and had dark cherry-colored eyes. He'd come down to the basement looking for us.

"How's young Dillinger?"

Talbot would invite him to sit on the trunk. I smiled, thinking of the booty under Bob. He told us about the

103

one arrest he'd made that week, a man from Stebbins Avenue who'd hurled his sister-in-law down the stairs. Bob liked to mock *The Blue Book of Crime.*

"Those FBIs think they're Sherlock Holmes. They do a lot of dusting for prints and they have an enormous crime lab. Edgar Hoover scratches on his violin and solves all the big cases. Bull. It's legwork and the number of canaries you keep."

"What kind of canaries?" I asked.

"Squealers," Talbot said. "Bob is talking about canaries that sing on their friends."

"Not only friends," Talbot said. "A good stoolie is worth a dozen street detectives."

"How many canaries do you have, Bob?"

"One or two."

It diminished Bob in my eyes, keeping canaries. But he lent us a certain authority. Even the roughest boys left us alone. We never paid a dime of tribute. That was because of Girlie as much as Bob.

I can't describe Girlie without going to Hollywood. She was a tall Carole Landis, a blonde Linda Darnell, covered with a veneer of flesh. The float of her hips was as mysterious as *The Blue Book of Crime.*

We'd grown up around Girlie and suffered because of that. She fed us sandwiches with her chest in my face. Talbot's mother worked, and so did mine. Girlie raised us. She was seven years older than Talbot. She'd finished high school in 1944, and though she planned to be an actress, Girlie sat at home. Bob would visit at irregular hours, hanging his policeman's hat on a hook behind the door. We envied him, of course, but we were careful of Bob's privacy. We intruded only once. We'd come back from softball in the park and hadn't seen Bob's hat on the door. He was lying on the living room sofa with Girlie's ankles around his neck. Her eyelids fluttered. She breathed like a swimmer, with great gulps of air.

I wondered when she'd elope with Bob. But Bob had a rival in Rosenquist, an assemblyman who was a power in the Bronx Democratic machine. Rosenquist had white hair and seemed ancient at thirty-five. His Lincoln Continental took up most of the block. He would court Girlie with yellow roses and a clean white shirt. He promised her Hollywood if she'd marry him. But Girlie was devoted to Bob. No assemblyman could have made Girlie gulp for air.

Bob would mope with us in the basement when Girlie was out in the Lincoln. We were dying to include him in our corporation. Talbot realized how valuable it would have been to have Young Dillinger & Co. under the kingdom of a cop's hat. We liked Bob and wanted him to woo Girlie with department-store gifts.

Still, I don't think Talbot should have opened the trunk. I would have hinted to Bob first what the corporation was about. But Talbot was relying on his genius and his genius failed. Bob looked at the display of merchandise and waltzed us to his precinct with the trunk on his back. Our mothers weren't home and our dads must have gone to a Yankee game with tickets from the Bronx machine. It was Girlie who released us. Bob rocked on his heels, trying to explain the circumstances.

"Girlie, I couldn't let them steal."

Girlie walked past him and out the precinct with Talbot, me, and Rosenquist. I could feel small explosions in her legs, and I knew that Girlie wasn't finished. She slapped at us with her hips. We hurtled down the block, drunk on perfume that wafted at us from behind Girlie's ear. It was like getting shoved by a gorgeous witch.

"Damn you," she said, soon as we were far enough from the police. "That locket you guys gave me, should I thank Mr. Sheridan for it? Bums, I washed your hair and went out in the middle of a storm, so you'd have mustard on your sandwiches."

"Leave them to me," Rosenquist said. "I'll make amends."

We arrived at Children's Court in Rosenquist's Lincoln Continental. He shook hands with court attendants, said hello to the judge. The courthouse was like a candy store where Rosenquist could pull ice cream sodas from the wall. Sheridan came with his department-store clerks. He was wearing a silver coat like some furrier out of Prague. None of his clerks would claim the goods from our trunk.

"That's nice," said the judge, who owed his livelihood to the Bronx machine. "Enough slippers and baseball mittens to field a team. Now where does that little treasure come from?"

106

Rosenquist stood up. "From the Quincy Adams Democratic Club, your honor. The boys did some work for us and the club showed its gratitude."

"Do you have affidavits to that effect?"

"Naturally," said Rosenquist, producing a sheaf of papers.

The judge frowned at Bob, who sat alone in his winter uniform.

"Silly business," said the judge. "Somebody's been wasting the court's precious time."

We had sponge cake at the Quincy Adams Club on Longfellow Avenue. The judge was there. Without his robe, he could have been a shoe salesman at Sheridan's store. Girlie was in a cocktail dress. Not one of the Democrats could take his eyes off her. Girlie's hair was swept back, and her neck looked carved from cantaloupe. She drank schnapps with the judge, her skin burning in the dark of the club.

Talbot didn't have to worry about spelling bees. He came down with a severe asthma attack and was sent to a school in Arizona. His people followed him there after six months. Rosenquist abandoned the Bronx machine to go with Girlie. He married her in Tucson.

Bob was transferred to City Island. His captain couldn't forgive him for involving the precinct in "a war with Quincy Adams." And so I was left with my mom and dad. Talbot wrote once or twice and then gave himself to Arizona. Girlie mailed her wedding picture to the Bronx. She wore another cocktail dress.

I became a sly character without Young Dillinger &

Co. Went to the City College and NYU Law, but I couldn't get that ideal of Girlie out of my head. I needed a blonde Linda Darnell.

Served my apprenticeship in that immense gulag of the Bronx District Attorney's office. And now I'm on permanent retainer to the Petrarch Brothers, Vincente and Charles, who have their own kingdom of call girls in Brooklyn and the Bronx. The Brothers pay me a fortune to look after their interests. I have bondsmen at my disposal and young lawyers to slug it out in court. Our cribs are hardly ever raided by the police. I don't have to spread money around. I play softball with the District Attorney's men. I instruct indigent clients for the Bronx machine. I can enter a judge's chamber without drawing an unkind stare. I'm the Brothers' gentleman attorney, the mob lawyer who memorized the whole of Talbot's vocabulary list.

I live with my dad near the Bronx Botanical Garden. My mother left us long ago for another man. My father still laments the loss of his billet as an air-raid warden. It's been years and years. Sometimes I entertain the notion of having him killed. I'd have to go to the Petrarchs, and I'm sure they'd consider patricide a bad risk. Suppose it got around that their lawyer had his own dad eliminated? The cops might get suspicious. Judges would scorn a Petrarch girl.

I'd have moved to Manhattan, set up housekeeping with Dad on Central Park West, but the Petrarchs like to have me in the neighborhood. We consummate our best deals inside the Botanical Garden, where every bush can't house a cop's microphone. Vincente calls me maestro, because I can spring a girl on all sorts of technicalities and skewer witnesses on the stand. I have a silver tongue, according to Charles.

He asked me to use that tongue in behalf of Marianne, a favorite of his. She's a madame on the Grand Concourse, tall and robust as Linda Darnell would have been if she hadn't died in a fire. I didn't have to jump into court for Marianne. Could have sent one of the lackeys from my office. But Marianne always made me think of Girlie. Her arrest had nothing to do with the Petrarchs. She wasn't on company business. She got into a fracas with a traffic cop and bit the cop's hand.

I gathered witnesses on the ride down to court, intending to use the old sexual gambit. I had a pair of widows and a pensioner to swear that the cop had tried to molest Marianne.

Ortiz was on the bench, a Quincy Adams man. He wouldn't protect a dumb traffic cop. "Children," I told my witnesses, "we have it made."

I whispered to Marianne about having dinner that night. The cop strolled in and paused at our table.

"Lawrence Tierney, is that you?"

My heart squeezed at the mention of Tierney. It was Bob, who'd been knocking around in a policeman's bag since 1946. Marianne watched us with crazed eyes. I asked Bob if he'd ever been married.

"No," he said.

And I knew. We'd both orphaned ourselves to Girlie. She existed as a lifelong ache.

"I'm sorry, kid," he said.

109

"Sorry about what?"

"That I got you into trouble."

"I've survived, Bob. Look at me. It was Talbot who had the asthma attack."

"Don't believe it."

"But he went to Arizona," I said.

"It was a scam. That assemblyman paid him to show me your treasure chest. He wanted Girlie and that was the only way to get her."

"You're bitter, Bob. Talbot would have mentioned something . . . we had a corporation to protect. He wouldn't have risked it for Rosenquist. Where did you learn that story?"

"From some Quincy Adams people. Ages ago. The assemblyman skipped to Arizona with a piece of the club's pie. The club couldn't tell you. People thought you were the canary Rosenquist left behind."

Ortiz knocked once with his hammer, assuming I had a bellyache. I didn't examine Bob on the stand. I didn't call our witnesses and Marianne got six months probation for biting Bob's hand.

She was furious. She begged Charles's permission to throw acid at his lawyer. I had ruined her reputation on account of a cop who was running traffic from his grave. Charles warned her. "Marianne, leave the maestro alone."

I sank into a melancholy during Marianne's probation period. Talbot had studied *The Blue Book* and swindled me. He was always the genius. I could imagine what *The Blue Book* said on the subject of friendship. "The most diabolic criminal minds have no room for friends. Their devotion is to pure technique."

I remembered Bob on the stand. In his late fifties now. With worn shoes. His face full of bloated handsomeness. Girlie's lover until the end.

I showed up at Marianne's crib with a bandolier of yellow roses. Marianne threw bottles of men's cologne at me and then laughed. "I can't hate you when you look so sad."

Charles called. "Maestro, I'm worried about you. Bringing flowers to a whore."

I spent six nights with Marianne and returned to my dad and the Bronx Botanical Garden. Two melancholics. Dad without his warden's hat and me without an ambience. I'm still Lawrence Tierney stealing from Sheridan's store. Merchandise had never been my strongest point. I was interested in the brotherhood of crawling on my belly with Talbot through a duct. If I fell down after Talbot and Girlie disappeared, I'm glad of that fall. I came into power thinking of her ankles around Bob's neck. I'd find Girlie's face in all the movies I ever saw. Where would I have been without the RKO? Carole Landis. Girlie. Linda Darnell.

One for the Money

PETER HEYRMAN

Peter Heyrman wrote "One for the Money" based on stories he overheard in Key West bars. He disavows the influence of Ernest Hemingway's To Have and Have Not, *which he did not read until after the first draft of "One for the Money" was written, and expresses some annoyance at being compared to Hemingway by editors, those at NBM not included. Mr. Heyrman has written two novels, one science fiction and the other a mystery, which are unpublished. He is thirty-two.*

SHADOWS MIXED with smoke in the palm fronds as the blades of the ceiling fan creaked. I sat and sweated at one end of the bar, as I admired the barmaid's figure. She was a fast-talking, funny girl named Nancy, but she wasn't talking too quickly that night. The July heat had sapped the energy out of everyone. The object of her attention was a gay waiter whose eyeshade was starting to melt.

Nancy smiled provocatively at him, but he didn't notice. He was busy running a wet tongue over his lips as he watched for pretty boys passing by on the street. When she tired of the lost cause she came down to where I was sitting. I lit a cigarette and gave her one. Smoke hung limp in the air between us.

"Any business lately?" she asked.

"Not much. I'll lay you out a line in the bathroom if you want."

"Okay. I need some energy."

Back in the bathroom I spread out cocaine on the top of the toilet tank, then chopped it to fine powder with my pocket knife. I made two lines, the larger one for her, then took my own. It rushed through my head, then spread over me like pins and needles. There was a knock at the door. I heard her laugh. As I opened it Nancy slipped past me. Once she'd snorted hers I grabbed her and kissed her. Her hands rubbed my back. When she let go she said,

"You've got business out there, lover."

"What kind of business?"

"The kind I worry about. Her name's Deborah."

"Why are you worried? Is she all right?"

"I guess so. Rick sent her. He called just now. Don't listen to me. She's waiting for you out there."

"You know her?"

"Uh-huh, and once you see her you won't be making so many passes at me."

I walked through drooping palm fronds to the dark bar. The woman was in the seat next to mine. She wore a white dress that stood out against the shadows.

She didn't look hot. She didn't even look mildly uncomfortable. As I sat down she slipped a cigarette into her mouth. I put my lighter up to it to get a better look at her face. It was something to see.

"I'm Mark Kane," I said.

"I'm Deborah."

"Nancy said you wanted to talk to me."

"Yes. Rick Gannet told me about you. He said you have a boat."

"I've got a thirty-one footer. She's not in the water now, but she will be in a week or so when I get the money to fix her."

"What's the trouble?"

"Just a couple of kinks in the engine. She could go in the water now, but she couldn't make a long haul."

Nancy approached us. "Would you like a drink, Miss Usher?"

Deborah Usher nodded, ordered, then turned back to me. "Could your boat get into the water any faster?"

"With money she could. I could go to Miami, get parts and have her ready by Friday. What's the rush?"

"There's a job if you'd like to take it."

"I'd need money right away."

"How much?"

"A thousand for parts, labor, all that. Expense money for an overnight stay in Miami."

"While we're up there we could stay at my apartment. I'll pay for your meals. Any other expenses we can take care of as we go."

I hadn't thought about her coming along, but I

114

didn't mind the idea. I figured I could handle her. "That'll be fine."

"You have a car?"

"Sure."

"We'll go up tomorrow, get the parts, and be back by Wednesday morning. Then could you be ready by Friday?"

"I don't see why not. What's the deal?"

"From what Rick told me you'll take it."

"Rick doesn't speak for me. I want to know what it is."

"Cocaine."

"I usually only deal in grass."

"But you've brought in cocaine."

"A couple of times. Never much of it."

"Can your boat go to Andros Island?"

"It can. It would take three days, maybe less."

"Three days is fine. I have a man who'll be going with you."

"I've got my own mate."

"That's all right, but my man will be with you. He knows the men you're meeting. You may know him. Keith is his name."

"Tall and bald?"

"Yes. He shaves his head."

"What's in it for me?"

"Forty pounds of cocaine."

My hand shook. I calculated quickly. Coke was going for twenty thousand a pound. "I'm interested. How much will I be carrying?"

"Five hundred pounds."

"I'd want three thousand bucks in advance in case anything goes wrong."

"That's fine. I'm staying at the Santa Maria, room 41. Will you pick me up tomorrow at two o'clock, and be ready to go to Miami?"

"All right."

She finished her drink, then faded into the dark.

Nancy appeared in front of me. "Another drink?"

"Yeah."

"You working for her?"

"I'm thinking about it."

"I wish you wouldn't."

I mulled that over for a while.

Nancy closed up at three-thirty. I waited for her as the last couple of stragglers melted into black heat. I caught her as she came out.

"Walk you home?"

"Sure."

We walked across Duval Street to Eaton, then turned east.

"What do you know about her?" I asked.

"She's okay."

"She won't screw me up?"

"I don't know. She always pays, and she's not a cop."

"What else?"

"Not a thing, Marky-boy."

We were at Nancy's door.

"You don't sound convincing," I told her.

"Mark, tell me one thing. Do you think about the things you do?"

"What kind of question is that?"

"It's a good question."

"I can't figure you out."

"You don't try hard enough."

I took hold of her, but she pushed me back lightly. "Not tonight, lover. You'll have to figure me out first."

"You want a line before bed?"

"No, thanks. See you, lover. Till next time, be careful." She disappeared through the doorway, leaving me standing in the heat. For a moment I felt like an ass, then I pulled the vial from my pocket and snorted some coke off a key. I remembered Deborah Usher and the money. White powder did its trick. I walked into a dream of streetlights and palm trees.

In the morning I searched for my first mate, Jimmy. I found him in a bar by the shrimp docks eating breakfast and drinking a beer.

"Drink in the morning at your age and you'll never get old like me," I told him.

He grinned. "I wouldn't if you could keep me busy." He fished in his pocket and pulled out a roll of antacid tablets.

"You shouldn't need those at your age either."

"If we were out fishing I wouldn't eat this goddamn greasy food."

"I'm getting the parts today."

"They came in?"

"I'm going to Miami to get them. You be ready to pull out Friday?"

"Sure. What's the deal?"

"More than we've ever done. A lot of coke."

"I don't know about coke. Is it close by?"

"Andros Island."

"That's a long way. Why not stick to grass?"

"We can quit it all after this. Your cut'll be a hundred thousand."

"Jesus! You sure?"

"If it works. I'll be paying you, and I'll have enough. Is a hundred thousand enough?"

"This is on the level?"

"Uh-huh. We have to take that guy Keith with us."

"That bald guy. I don't know."

"For this much money you don't know?"

"Okay, okay. Who's doing all this?"

"I'll let you know later. For now are you in?"

"A hundred thousand? I've got to be. Just make sure it's okay, Mark."

"Don't worry, Jimmy. It's my ass too. I'll meet you at the boat at five tomorrow afternoon. She's got to be ready by Friday."

"How long will we be out?"

"Six or seven days. This one will set us up."

"I'm ready."

I left him to his beer, checked the boat, and by two o'clock I was knocking on Deborah's door. She answered right away.

"Come in."

The motel room was no different from any other: a double bed, a desk bolted to the wall, bad paintings, and a shag carpet. There was a suitcase, and a notebook by the phone, but not one other personal effect was in sight.

"I talked to my first mate. He'll do it. We've got to be back by five tomorrow afternoon so he and I can get to work."

"That'll be fine. Sit down. Would you like a drink?"

"Maybe we ought to get going." She stepped behind me. I felt long fingers on my shoulders. The skin on her fingers was soft, but there was something in her touch that felt like a steel grip.

"We have a little time." She drew me onto the bed. We didn't leave until a half hour later. She sat next to me in the car surveying the world through dark-green glasses.

"I wasn't really expecting that," I said.

"What?" she laughed.

"Bed."

"Why not? You're not bad-looking."

"I still didn't expect it."

"I wanted to find out something about you."

"What did you find?"

"I found enough."

I stopped quizzing her. We drove up the island highway, and got to Miami at six. As we neared the city I drove by the warehouse where the parts were. They were just closing, but we got in the door. I had what I needed in a few minutes. As I loaded it in the trunk I said:

"We could go back now, and I could get an early start on it."

"There's no hurry."

We ate at a small Italian place, drinking cheap red wine with our spaghetti. Her eyes softened in candlelight, but that was just the shadows.

"You like living in this town?" I asked her.

"It's living."

"Maybe to some people. I can't stand it here."

"But you do like Key West?"

"It'll do. It's a little more peaceful."

"It doesn't matter much where you live, it's how you live. I like to live well. That takes money. The money is here, not in Key West."

"Still, you come there for a boat."

"I go a lot of places for a lot of things."

"How long have you been here?"

"A couple of months."

"Where are you from?"

"Nowhere in particular. I was once married to a man from South America. He had a large estate, but even then we traveled most of the time."

"What happened to him?"

"He died, leaving me a lot of unfinished business. You ask too many questions."

"I like to know about my business partners."

"You're not my partner. You're doing a job for me."

"Anyway you want to look at it, lover."

She smiled, and stubbed her cigarette into the ashtray. "It's time to go."

Her place showed she liked to live well. It was a penthouse. The stereo was in the five-figure price range, and the TV took up most of a wall. She had plenty of tapes to watch, but I preferred watching her. She took me straight to the bedroom and gave me a guided tour of herself. When she dozed I stayed awake. I watched a tape of an old Barbara Stanwyck thriller. When it ended I had a drink and looked around her room. Except for the tapes and records, there was nothing personal there. Everything was modern, clean, and cold. The look of the room sliced the eye. I shrugged it off and got in bed, but it took me a while to sleep.

In the morning we had more fun and games. She was an acrobat. There was a moment when I thought I could stay with her forever, but the moment passed. A short while after that we were driving south. Two hours later we were on the Keys, where we stopped at a greasy spoon for breakfast.

"This isn't exactly style," I said of our surroundings. The place stank of Lysol and bacon grease.

"It'll do." She reached for an English muffin. "When I'm on the road I kind of like places like this. They remind me of when I was a kid. My dad and I traveled, and we always ate in places like this."

"Where's your dad now?"

"Dead."

"I'm sorry."

"Don't be. He's better off that way."

I shut up and finished my coffee. As we drove back to Key West she laid out the deal. Basically I was a transporter. Keith would handle all the business.

"Where did you hook up with him?" I asked.

"I can always find the people I want."

"If you've got the money to work something like this, why do you stay so close to it?"

"What do you mean?"

"I know guys who are small-time compared to this, but they keep their distance from the real nuts and bolts of a deal."

"I like it. It's a thrill."

"What if things get rough?"

"I'm too lucky for that." She said it coldly, but to me it sounded naive. The rest of the way we made small talk. When we got to her motel she slipped her arms around me, and I felt the ice grip of her fingers again.

"Do you like me, Mark?"

"A lot."

"This doesn't have to be the last job you do for me."

I thought about my plans to quit, then I thought about the girl who held me. She let go and got out of the car. I didn't wave good-bye.

That night was the night when Nancy said to me, "Marky-boy's going to learn a few things on this one."

She said it as she set a cold beer in front of me. The bar was empty, and the long line of stools looked lonely. Most people were home lying in front of fans that blew the sweat off them.

"Why do you say that?" I asked.

"Because I know the kind of woman she is. She teaches men, the hard way. I saw her with that bald-headed man, Keith, today. Is he working with you?"

"You see a lot of things," I said quietly. "Maybe you shouldn't watch so much."

"What do you mean?"

"I don't want you mixed up in it."

"Then maybe you shouldn't be mixed up in it either. Have you slept with her yet?"

"What the hell does that have to do with it?"

She got up and walked down to one of the liquor shelves. She started dusting off the bottles even though they didn't need it. "I won't say anything more about it."

She kept her promise, and we sat in the hot silence for another half hour. By that time it was three o'clock.

"I'm closing now," she said as she locked up the liquor cabinets.

"I'll walk you home."

"If you want."

When we got to her house she kissed me, and kept her arms loosely around my neck. "I wish you'd never seen her, Mark. I like you too much to wish anything else."

"I don't get you."

"If I explained you wouldn't hear me."

"Can I come in? We'll talk about it."

"Not tonight. Maybe when you get back, if you have time for me then."

She kissed me again, then broke out of my arms and

vanished into shadows. For a few moments I thought about Nancy, but it didn't last long. Another woman took over my mind, and she wouldn't let go.

On Friday morning the boat was in the water. Jimmy stocked her while I drove to Deborah's motel for last-minute instructions. Keith was with her when I got there. He grunted as he opened the door. He didn't smile. When Deborah came out of the bathroom she didn't bother with greetings.

"Can you get there by Monday night?"

"I don't see why not. You have my money?"

"Yes." She took out a roll of hundreds, then counted out three thousand. She started making another pile. Keith held up his hand.

"You keep it for me. I won't need it out there."

"You should have something," she said.

"I already do."

She almost smiled. I tried to wear a deadpan as I pocketed my money. Deborah spoke in a monotone as she told us what to look for off Andros.

"From there it's up to you," she finished. Keith nodded, opened the door, and stepped out. When he was outside I took her shoulders and kissed her hard.

"I'll see you when you get back," she whispered. "Be careful."

I looked into her eyes. She softened them. I watched her lips as her tongue licked them. I let her go and walked out, not wanting to see any change in that picture. I didn't know if she was real, and I wasn't about to let myself care. I just wanted a memory to try to

124

come back to, even if it were a brittle photograph that would crumble at the touch.

Keith was waiting in the car. I noticed all he had was a small suitcase. Well, I thought, he doesn't travel like a sailor. I wondered how he liked the sea. He looked like a passenger about to board to cruise ship. All he needed was a camera.

"Why's he with us?" Jimmy asked, wiping white powder from an antacid tablet off his lips. We'd been at sea for a couple of hours, and we'd just passed the Torch Keys.

"She wanted him here. He's setting it up."

"He's too quiet. Gets on board, goes right down to sleep. Does he know anything about boats?"

"No. It's all up to you and me on that count."

"Fine with me."

Jimmy took the helm for a while as I sat back and worked on my tan. I was asleep in a few minutes. When the sun got low Jimmy woke me and I took her. A half hour later, as dusk filled water and sky, Keith came up. He stood next to me, gazing off the bridge.

"You're doing well out of this," he said.

"Well enough."

"It's the one you've been waiting for. I've looked around. I know."

"Yeah, you know. So what? What are you getting?"

"Money. Otherwise I'm not sure. Perhaps you feel the same way."

"You mean about Deborah."

"Deborah." He sucked on that word, then lit a cigar.

125

He threw the match away, thrust his bald head up, and looked at the sky. "You went to Miami with her. You got what I want."

"I got what I got. Look, right now we have a job. Money's what we both want, and between us we can get it."

"Then we'll get back." He smiled and smoked.

"I'm not worried about it."

"You think it will be that easy?"

"I didn't say that, but I'm not so worried about it. She's only a woman." I wondered if that was what she was.

"Ha. She is a smart woman. She has hired us, has she not, and set us into positions which bring a certain, measured pressure."

"I'm not pressured."

"No? This deal can treat you very well. A couple more can treat you even better. A few, and you own the world. As long as you get by the IRS, you will live in style for the rest of your life. Like her."

"If I'm like her, I'll be keeping my fingers in the dirty work."

"Yes, she likes that. That's what I admire. She doesn't have to do it this way, but she enjoys it. Do you enjoy it, Mr. Kane?"

"I do what I have to do."

"That's no way to get a woman like her. For her you must do more."

"You go ahead and do more. I want to get the job done."

He took a long drag from his cigar, then climbed below chuckling. He was back a half hour later not looking so sure of himself.

"Have you listened to the radio, Mr. Kane?"

"Not lately."

"There's a squall line coming through the Gulf, traveling fast, thirty-knot winds and high seas. They're putting out warnings."

"They are, are they. I heard about them. They might catch us, but we'll handle them. Jimmy and I have been through worse."

That smoothed his worry wrinkles. "They might not hit us."

"They might blow themselves out. If not you can stick it out below, but if you puke use your hat."

He frowned and went below. Jimmy came up a minute later. "What's with Keith?"

"I get the feeling he doesn't like the sea."

"That's not hard to tell."

Jimmy took her while I went to get some shut-eye. Sleep didn't come easy. Every time I felt a dream approaching, Deborah Usher got up and stood in the way of it, then I'd open one eye and see the moon rising out of the soup of the sea. The moon and Deborah Usher; both hard, cold, and bright.

At three in the morning Jimmy shook me awake. He was sweating despite the cool breeze.

"I'm not feeling so good. Think you could take her for a while?"

"Sure, Jimmy. What's the problem?"

"Just something in my stomach. It comes and goes. A couple of hours' sleep and I'll be fine."

"Okay. You need anything, just yell."

I went back up. Keith was sprawled on a deck recliner, his bald head lying against the back of the chair like a watermelon. On the bridge I checked the course. It was fine, so I sat back and stared at the stars. I thought about the hundred thousand Jimmy was getting. It wasn't enough. The boy was risking too much, and I decided he ought to get more. Still, I couldn't cut him in on the cocaine. He wouldn't know what to do with it. Those thoughts went by as the air rushed over me, and the boat cut the water of the Florida Straits. I was almost dozing when Keith climbed onto the bridge. He still looked nervous.

"Have you heard any more about the storms?"

"I think they're still west of the Keys. They won't be a problem. A lot of squall lines take a turn toward Cuba. Even if this one doesn't, we'll outrun it. Just be glad we aren't going the other way."

"I am." He relaxed and pulled out a cigar. He lit it and blew smoke into the wind. "This is a charter boat, is it not, Mr. Kane?"

"Yeah, it is."

"Do you still take out charters?"

"Not much anymore."

"Why not? Don't you like it?"

"I used to. I still like to fish, and I do that enough. I got tired of charters, though. They don't give a damn

128

about fishing. They just want to take a trophy home. They get drunk and talk about real estate and other guys' wives while you do the work. Charters stink."

"But after this trip you won't have to worry about that anymore."

"After this I might as well go up north. Not too far north, just far enough to find a lake. Someplace where I can live easy and catch a few bass. I might like that kind of fishing better."

"You'd miss it, Mr. Kane."

"Miss what?"

"Late nights, bars, drugs."

"Maybe, maybe not."

"The women."

I shut up.

"How many women do you get, Mr. Kane?"

"Goddamn you, don't start throwing Deborah in my face again."

"Are you afraid to talk about her?"

I swung around and grabbed his collar. "Lay off, dammit. We're going to be a week together on this boat. Don't give me any crap."

"Finally you react."

I pushed him away from me. "The hell with you."

"I simply want an idea of where I stand. She is so uncommunicative about certain things. I thought you might help me understand."

"Get back down on the deck. We won't talk about this anymore."

"But—"

129

"I'm ordering you." He did what I told him. I checked the course, lit a cigarette, then watched the night pass. As the moon slid down the west side of the sky I felt as if it were keeping an eye on me.

It was almost sunrise when I heard the scream. It came from beneath me. Keith was coming out of his deck chair. His eyes were like matches in the thin light. The scream sounded again. I scrambled for the cabin. Jimmy lay writhing on his bunk. I grabbed him, then held him down. His forehead was as hot as the top of a fired-up stove. He squirmed as if he wanted to crawl out of his skin.

Keith stood blank-faced in the portal. "Get me ice," I barked.

"All right."

He disappeared, then came back with a bag of nine or ten cubes. I pressed them onto Jimmy's forehead. His body relaxed a little.

"You okay?" I whispered. At first he didn't answer. He was gulping air. Finally he nodded. "It's your stomach, right?"

"And sides," he groaned.

"Put some ice on his right side," Keith said.

"Why?"

"Is his right side hard?"

I felt there. "Yes."

"That's where he will need it."

I put the ice against his side. "What else do I do?"

"Nothing."

130

I didn't like the tone of his voice. "Okay, go on up, Keith. I'll be there in a minute." Keith left. I heard his footsteps going to the bridge.

"Does it still hurt?"

"Yeah, but not as bad. I'll be okay. I don't know what hit me."

"Whatever it was, it hit you pretty hard. Now get some sleep. If you need anything yell. I'll be back in a few minutes."

I went to the bridge. Keith stared over the bow. "So what's wrong with him?" I asked.

"Appendicitis. Acute, if I don't miss my guess."

"How do you know?"

"I was a medic in the service. I worked in a hospital in Da Nang. I saw a few cases like this."

"What'll happen to him?"

"If he doesn't die right away, he'll have more attacks. They'll get longer, and the intervals between them will shorten. We might keep him going with a lot of ice and water, but it won't be long before an attack kills him. The appendix will rupture . . ."

"Then?"

"Yes, then he dies. How's our water supply?"

"I always bring more than I need, but if he's going to need a lot, I don't know."

"It's something to think about, isn't it? Do you really need him?"

"I need him all right."

"I can manage the boat when it's calm, and you can rest then. If it gets rough I can call you."

I eyed him. I was slow to see his meaning. Who would watch over Jimmy while I slept? Then I figured it out.

I turned the boat over to Keith. "We'll see how you do. Take her for a minute. I want another look at him."

I went down to the cabin. Jimmy lay there looking like a shimmering apparition. His body was exhausted and shiny with sweat. He was sleeping. I opened a drawer, took out my gun, and checked it. It was loaded. There were catlike footsteps on the deck. I moved quietly to the entry. I saw his shadow, then him. He held a gun. As he passed me I said,

"Drop it. I've got one too." He let the gun slip, turned, then smiled. Jimmy didn't wake. "Get back up there, Keith." I followed him. Once we were on the bridge he was polite as hell.

"Mr. Kane, is this a game?"

"If it is, you're losing it."

"What are you thinking about me?"

"I'm thinking you want to kill him."

"Not necessarily. We could simply let him die."

"Wrong. We're turning back. We're taking him to Miami. It's no more than twelve hours from here."

"You forget. We have to go through the storm if we turn around."

"You're scared of that, aren't you? Don't worry, buddy, you'll get a real good look at it, one you can write home about."

"But what about your friend? He won't last through it."

The air was still. "He'll make it. He's a tough kid.

And since you're such a fine medic, you're going to help him. You're going to tell me everything I should do for him."

"Why should I? After all, you're robbing me of a fortune."

"You'll do it because if he dies you die."

"You're insane. We can get to Andros. There must be a hospital there."

"That's a day and a half away. Sorry, Keith. We're staying poor."

Keith looked sick. "When we get back I won't take the blame. She'll want a scapegoat, you know."

"No, she won't. She'll see it my way. She'll have to."

I went below, then returned with some rope. "Sit in the deck chair," I told him.

"Why?"

"I need your help on something. Unless you want me to fire this, you're going to sit down." When he sat I tossed him two lengths of rope. "Tie your feet to the chair."

"You think I'm going to tie myself up?"

"I'm aiming at your heart. Make the knots tight, not fancy ones, just good square knots. I'll check your work later."

I watched him work. "Sit back and tie one around your chest." He did it loosely. "Tighter. Now put one over your neck. Tie it in the back."

"I can't see what I'm doing."

"I can. You're doing fine." I went behind him, put the gun beside me, then put my arm around his neck. "If you try grabbing for me, I'll have the leverage, so

133

don't try it." He tried. I squeezed his neck hard. He quit. "Put your hands on the frames before I blow your head off." I tied his hands, then checked his other knots. He was no Boy Scout, but the knots were good.

"You're going to tell me everything you know about taking care of the kid." He took his time, but finally he'd choked out the instructions. I wrote them down, then got a beer, and went to the bridge to change course. I headed for Miami. I checked the radio. I was too far away to transmit, but I heard more on the squalls.

They were aimed at us.

The sun climbed the sky, and the waves started churning. I tried to call shore, or the Coast Guard, but got no answer. I heard a lot though. The patrols were chasing small craft out of the water.

"You're not bringing police into this," Keith shouted.

"They can get him in quicker."

"They're going to ask a lot of questions, maybe search us."

"I'm clean."

Keith looked more worried than he ought to be. At first I thought it was the storm, but then I pondered it more. Deborah had said the money was taken care of, but she hadn't said how. Someplace on board was more money than I'd ever seen.

I climbed down to the deck. "Where's the money, Keith?"

"What?"

"It's got to be here. You had a suitcase when you boarded. How the hell did you fit that much cash in it though?"

"It's not money. It's not anything you can use, Kane. It's papers, deeds, and all that. She's signed them, but they won't help you. You're out of luck."

"Sounds like a risky way to do business."

"They represent property outside the U.S. They'll be no help to you, but they could hurt her if they fell into the wrong hands."

"Why didn't you tell me about them when I tied you up?"

"I thought you would come to your senses. We could still turn around. There's time. He won't make it, Kane. He—"

A yell burned my ears. I ran in and found Jimmy flailing like a rabid animal. His mouth snapped open and closed. I grabbed him, shoving a metal pen in his mouth so he wouldn't bite his tongue off. I kept a grip on him. The pen flew from his mouth, followed by a gush of vomit. He heaved again, then started convulsing. I thought I would lose him, but then he started to quiet down. I felt his right side. It was stone. I iced it as he oozed sweat. Tears filled his eyes.

"Can you talk?"

"I—I shit myself."

"Take it easy. I'll clean you up." I got him fresh underwear, then turned the mattress and changed the sheets while he slumped in a chair. The boat began to

135

pitch. Outside the sun was gone. I got Jimmy into bed. "How do you feel?"

"Not good. I don't know how I'm going to make it, Mark."

"You'll make it. You've got to. This might be the most expensive recovery in history, so you better get your money's worth. Did you see where Keith put his suitcase?"

"The cabinet, there." He pointed to it.

"Thanks. Now that squall's coming up. After that we'll get you on a Coast Guard boat, and they'll get you to Miami quick, but I'm going to have to tie you down in the meantime, or you might get hurt."

"I know." He didn't seem to care much. I got his hands and feet where I wanted them, then made the loops as comfortable and loose as I could. I lined his side with ice, then got the suitcase and climbed on deck.

"Do you have the key?" I asked Keith. He let out a whine. "Look, if you want I'll pitch it overboard, but I thought I'd save you the suitcase. I'm a considerate bastard."

"She'll kill us, Kane. Can't you see that?"

"She won't kill me." I went through his pockets and found the key. The deeds were in the case. They were to property in Peru.

"Is this the land where they grow it?" I asked.

"Yes. She's in trouble. She can only get the crop by giving up the land. I'm not sure why, but she's scared. She'll kill us.'

136

"If I know the Coast Guard, she'll have to wait awhile. I'm sure they'll cook up some reason to keep us for a few days."

"She'll wait. She still has a lot of cash. She can wait."

"The hell with her." I tossed the papers overboard. As wind scattered them Keith let out a howl worse than Jimmy's. The boat rocked badly. I took my last length of rope.

"I'll tie down the chair so you won't go overboard." He didn't thank me for it. I checked the rest of the boat, threw his gun off the side, then tried the radio once more. I got through. The Coast Guard told me to sit tight, they'd be out.

"Not much else I can do," I said. As the storm worsened I climbed to the bridge, then ignored everything but rain, sea, and boat. The waves grew mean, and rain spat on me. I heard the main part of the storm roaring over the sea. Then it was there.

The rain was thick enough to hide the bow, and the wind wanted to take me off the wheel. It was a roar in the ears, water slapping the face and forcing the eyes closed. It was a boat that rolled like a seesaw, trying to tear out the stomach. It was weightless, howling, flooding. I tried to become a part of the shifting sea surface, to float, to stay where there was still air to breathe. After a while the rain slackened, and the wind stopped trying to rip my ears away. The waves rolled, but they began to ebb. I could see again, and the bow was still there. That's when I felt the sap hit.

It wasn't a clean hit, and I went for my gun. That's

where his hand was going. I jumped away quickly, and held the gun on him. He wasn't moving too well on the swaying boat.

"The boy's probably dead by now," he hissed. "If not he will be."

"How'd you get out of the ropes?"

"The chair frame broke. It freed my hand. I'm throwing him over, Kane. He's not going to make it."

"If he's still alive he'll make it."

"You'll have to kill me to stop me. You're too smart for that."

"I'm stupid as hell."

"Dammit! We can still get there. We're in international waters, and we've got a head start on the Coast Guard. When we get there, we'll work it out. Deborah can send copies of the papers. We might have to cut in a messenger, but those men will wait for us. We can do it, Kane."

"You're crazy."

"Once he's overboard you'll have to come with me, or explain it to the Coast Guard. If you kill me, you'd have to explain that too."

He backed down toward the deck.

"You go near that cabin and I'll kill you."

"If you do, you'll go to jail. The boy won't be a witness, and I'm unarmed. They'll see it that way. I'll let you have Deborah, if you can get her. You probably can. She wants you anyway. And you'll be away from those stinking charters, and all of this rotten business. You'll have money and the woman. You won't shoot."

138

The gun trembled. It was growing too heavy to hold up. I started to lower it. He took a step. The world exploded.

The Coast Guard got there ten minutes later, and took Jimmy and Keith away. The paramedic told me Jimmy would make it. He wasn't conscious, and he didn't wake for two days. It was touch and go, but he pulled through. Still, it was as Keith had predicted, but worse. Jimmy didn't remember a thing, and the cops weren't impressed.

They didn't like it largely because of their other passenger. Keith had a hole in his belly about the size of a cue ball. I'd tried to stop the bleeding, but it was impossible. Besides, I had Jimmy to attend to. Keith was still alive when the Coast Guard got there, and he stayed alive for several hours. He even told them about the trip, and with his last ounce of strength he signed a statement he'd dictated. Then he conveniently died. The statement said I'd shot him in an argument over a bet. We'd wagered on whether Jimmy was going to die, with me on the side of death.

They gave me an attorney, and he visited me one day.

"We haven't got much to work with," he said, "not unless you open up."

"I've opened up all I can. We were taking a cruise. Jimmy got sick, so we came back. Keith didn't like Jimmy, hated his guts, I don't know why. He tried to push him overboard. He was going to try again, so I killed him."

139

"It won't go over."

"I know it."

"So why not tell me the truth?"

"Hell, it's as true as any other story I'd give you. I'm not sure what the truth is."

"You're a hell of a client. You're protecting people. The cops know what you were doing out there, but they can't prove it, so they're going to sweat it out of you, or fry you."

"If I could tell them what they want to hear, what would happen?"

"What would it be?"

"I'd have to think about that."

"You might get off the murder charge. They might make it manslaughter or less. But whatever you said would have to be good."

"Forget it. There's nothing else anyway."

"Okay, then I'll tell you: We can probably get you off on second-degree murder. You'll be looking at a fifteen-year sentence. You might get out in four if you're lucky."

"If it happens, it happens."

Jimmy told me later that they'd questioned him too. He tried to remember anything that might help, but they kept poking holes in his story. Still, they couldn't pin anything on him. Deborah's name never came up. I got stuck with twelve years, but I might be out in three.

Jimmy visits now and then. So does Nancy. She smiles a lot, and kisses me through the screen. She

140

says she's waiting for me to get out. Sometimes I believe it. Sometimes I have to.

Then yesterday I had a new visitor. The guard brought me out, and I walked down the aisle past other prisoners as I stared at the other side of the screen. It was Deborah. She was as beautiful as ever, but she seemed jumpy. Something had happened in her eyes.

"Hi, Deborah."

"Hello."

"Thanks for coming." She didn't say anything for a while, so I spoke up again. "I like looking at you. Was that why you came? Or were you just in the neighborhood?"

"You never told them, did you?"

"No."

"I should feel something for that. Did you really kill him?"

"Yes."

"Maybe you should've told them everything. If you had, you might not be here."

"Oh, I'd be here. So would you. And Jimmy would, too."

"That's right, your mate. Did Keith talk to you about me?"

"Yeah, a few times."

"Is that why you killed him?"

"No."

She looked disappointed. "He didn't really know me."

"Neither did I," I said.

141

"Nobody does."

She was quiet, then we said a few inanities. Finally she said, "When you get out, find me. I've still got money, and I've got—"

"I know what you've got, and I want it, but I'll get it somewhere else, thanks. I want it right now, but even if I could have it I wouldn't want the price tag. Since when did you make it your business to get horny guys in prison to think you're waiting for them, legs open?"

"I'm glad you're here," she hissed. "I hope they keep you."

She left, and the guard took me back to the cell. That's where I am now, and maybe they will keep me forever, until I am the cell, until I am the bars, the bare light bulb, and the newspaper whose gray print tells me she put a bullet in her head last night. It had been a beautiful head, but when she'd left her eyes had been flat, not icy like they used to be. She'd been in a cell too, one worse than mine, and finally she'd found the only way out. I look at four walls.

Who keeps the key?

The Death of the Tenth Man

STEVE OREN

Steve Oren was born in New York and lives in Chicago. After an academic career as a political scientist, he joined the civil service. "The Death of the Tenth Man," is his first published fiction. Kaddish has over the centuries evolved into, among other things, a memorial prayer. A Jew recites it in the eleven months following the death of either parent, and on the anniversary of the death. Even Jews who ignore many other customs observe this. Kaddish, a public prayer, may only be recited if a minyan (ten Jewish males over the age of 13) is present. As we see here, getting a minyan together is not always easy.

YOU HAVE TO PAY to belong to a family. I'm paying. It's 8:10 A.M. Sunday morning. And I'm in synagogue. Dale (but remember to call him Dovid to his face) called on Thursday.

"You know, Sunday is the anniversary of Dad's death."

"Yeah. I also know the word yahrzeit. But Sunday is a work day for me. This refugee thing..."

"Look, you do nothing else Jewish. You're still Dad's son." Did I hear or imagine the words "even if you married that shiksa?" "Besides, they've been having trouble getting a minyan. See you in shul Sunday morning." So that's why he was so polite. I only imagined the words.

Well. Dale—Dovid—had been right enough. He glares from the front of the shul, where he's leading the prayers. Either of us could have, but I'm not interested. We're up to "Omer Rebbe Yishmael." The first kaddish in memory of Dad should be a minute away. There are only nine men.

"Say, Mr. Greenberg, did you call your son?"

"Now, Dovid, he promised me he'd be here. Besides, Ann is ill and I don't like to disturb her with calls. Look, keep on davening until 'Yishtabakh.' If Joe isn't here by eight-fifteen or so, I'll call."

Aside from Dovid, no one seems concerned. At this shul, no longer able to afford a rabbi, in an area that has lost most of its Jews—in which many of my clients lived—lacking a tenth man must be fairly commonplace. But Moe and Hymie have turned backward to look at the outside door. Roger sleeps. Five years ago, the first time Dale dragged me back here (after Pao-Chu and I split), Roger was sleeping. Of course, he knows no Hebrew, doesn't pray, and comes only as a favor to Mr. Greenberg. Mr. Abrams also seems to be sleeping. Huddled in his big brown coat, the hood over his head, he is almost invisible. Last year, he hadn't slept. He cursed the cold, especially in the toilets, and the kidney condition that made him visit them constantly. Is he wearing tefillin? Can't tell with that coat over his head. Last year, Dale had hocked him. "Don't wear tefillin if you're going to wet your pants every five minutes."

"Barukh Sheomar," calls Dovid. I face forward and pick up a siddur. I'm here, might as well look at the old prayerbook. After a few minutes, my attention wanders.

Brown in the corner of my eye must be Mr. Abrams. I half-turn to watch the coat, reaching to the ankles, walk up the aisle. Moe and Hymie have also turned. " 'Bye, Jake." No answer. We exchange greetings for a minute or two. Then, as Dovid continues to drone on, I turn forward and they again face the rear.

Funny how someone you knew when you were a kid, especially someone you disliked when you were a kid and he an adult, you can't think of him by a first name. Moe and Hymie Bernstein are as old as Mr. Abrams and Mr. Greenberg. Dale and I are the only men here under seventy. But when I was a kid, Moe and Hymie Bernstein went to Anshe Emunah two blocks away.

Eventually, Mr. Greenberg stands up. He shuffles slowly toward the office.

"Good morning, Mrs. Abrams, how are you? I've got to call Ann about Joe."

This would be a long morning. Joe lives, or lived last year, in Northtown, thirty minutes' drive away. I do have an office to run. At "Yishtabakh" there was still

145

no minyan. Mr. Greenberg announces that Joe had overslept but would be here shortly. Roger sleeps. The other men talk. Dovid again glares, since talking is really not proper.

I like talking—that's how anthropologists make a living. But I see these men maybe once a year and have little to say. And why make Dale mad? He belongs in this shul as little as I do. The other men pray in an Orthodox shul out of cultural familiarity. He is Orthodox by conviction. They are retired shopkeepers with little Jewish knowledge, and most of that is wrong. He is a computer programmer and an ordained rabbi. In East Simonson Heights, among other religious professionals, he can relax a bit. Here he is on guard, the champion of Jewish law. And I'm here: the twin who went in the opposite direction. He would not eat in the house of any man here. None of them would have eaten in mine while Pao-Chu was there.

Five minutes, ten minutes. I find a Bible on the shelf and start translating the Hebrew to myself. Moe and Hymie continue to look toward the rear, facing the door. There are footsteps on the outside stairs. The door opens. "Hi, Joe" comes a chorus. Joe comes in the door, takes off his coat and hat, puts a yarmulke on his head, and walks from the corridor into the shul. He's balding—just as I am starting to. But he's still very tall. He was on our yeshiva high school basketball team. Dovid starts to lead the service.

"Roger, wake up, it's time for 'Borokhu.' Wait, Dovid, there's still no minyan. Where's Abrams?"

146

I'm tired of sitting in one place. "I'll get him," I say and walk out. To my left, I see Mrs. Abrams in the office, a ball in a coat. She's far more religious than her husband, at least she was twenty years ago. But going into the women's section of the shul to pray is something she does only on Saturday morning. If she has to drive her husband here on Sunday, she avoids the comparatively warm shul and stays in the office reading last week's Yiddish newspaper. But she doesn't count for the minyan. I'm supposed to get her husband.

I turn right toward the stairway that goes to the basement. From my right eye, I see Dovid pointing to the boxes on his left arm and head, reminding me not to wear my tefillin into the toilet. Down the stairs to the first landing. The side door is heavily bolted. I reach the basement and put out my hand to turn on the light. As it goes on, I see Mr. Abrams on the floor. There's a knife in his chest. Dovid will be disappointed.

But he wasn't. When we called, the detectives came pretty promptly. One of them was Bernie Gold. After some discussion about the propriety of praying with Mr. Abrams's body in the building, we had our minyan after all. The paramedics sedated Mrs. Abrams and led her out of the office. It became a police headquarters. After the police spoke to me and the others, Mr. Greenberg came over.

"This is terrible, Mike, just terrible."

"Yes, Mr. Greenberg." I'm twelve years old again.

"Mr. Abrams was such a fine man." I'm silent. "Came to shul every day. You know, he knew your dad well. Such a shame. Your father was always so proud of this shul and the neighborhood. Now, it's changed. Lots of shwartzes." He means Indians and Latinos as well as blacks. There are few blacks around here. Mr. Greenberg's prejudices are simple. The world contains Jews, goyim, and shwartzes. Jews can do no wrong except by acting like goyim. Goyim you mumble about. Shwartzes are bad. "Must have been one of them."

"How? No one was in the basement. The police have looked. And the only door was bolted from the inside."

"He must have sneaked out through the main door. These schwartz kids are sneaky, a bunch of shkotzim."

"Moe and Hymie were watching the back door the whole time." He is obviously not listening to me. Bernie Gold is heading toward me. He waves me to a side.

"Thanks, Bernie."

"Been a long time, Mike. Looks like Mr. Greenberg hasn't changed. You, me, and your brother—the silvers and the gold."

"Sure has. How did a sixties radical become a policeman?"

"Long story. It's hard to remember. Maybe I was never that much of a radical."

I bet. You were just radical enough that you went to Canada. Stayed there, I suspect, until the Carter

148

amnesty. Dovid was just religious enough to study in a yeshiva after high school. But in his case it stuck. You're a cop. He's a computer programmer. And I went to Vietnam. A Vietnam combat veteran who has just been next to a murder. I can guess the next question, especially as Bernie gets his friendly smile together.

"Did you have any reason to kill Jake Abrams?"

"Sure. Twenty-five years ago. So did you and every other kid in this shul."

"That I remember." He's lost his smile as he recalls the slaps Mr. Abrams gave to any kid who talked near him during prayer. Our fathers didn't hit us like that. But when we complained they reminded us that we shouldn't be talking.

I fill Bernie in on the years since 1968. I'm very careful to stress my graduate degree in anthropology—Jews are suckers for intellectuals—and the fact that I'm teaching part-time at the university. I also mention my refugee-relief job. As a Vietnam vet, I'm a success. Bernie hears the defensive tone.

"Look, Mike, I'm not reading you your rights or anything. But we've talked to everyone except Mrs. Abrams, who's a wreck. Someone killed Jake Abrams after he left this room. No one is in the basement. The only way to get into or out of it is to go through the corridor, which the Bernstein boys, and the rest of you from time to time, were watching to see if anyone would come to make your minyan." Bernie is still traditional. Moe and Hymie Bernstein never married.

Seventy-five years old they may be, but boys they remain. "Then Joe walked directly in. And then you went down those stairs."

"Fingerprints?" I know the answer but ask anyway.

"Yeah, you and the lab. It's the shul's knife. There are fifty years of fingerprints and shmutz on it."

"Okay. But I didn't kill him. If you don't mind, it's noon and I've got work to do. When can I get out of here?"

"The boss says all of you can go. Just don't go too far. Anyway, I'm sure Dale wants a minyan here for minkha this afternoon. See you at five."

"Thanks, Bernie." But no thanks. I spent lots of time thinking up an excuse for minkha. And if I show up, Dale will invite me to supper. Will he be more unhappy if I accept or if I decline? Last year there was a near riot when I let slip in front of his kids the news that Dad, their venerable grandfather, the fount of orthodoxy, had worked every Saturday in his store.

I take my coat from the rack, it's next to the big brown one, and put it on. Dale is talking to Bernie. "Autopsy," "sense of Jewish obligation" come through the air. Bernie looks unhappy. The other men are watching me. As soon as I leave, I will be the topic of conversation. I'm out the door, walking through sodden fall leaves to my car.

The office is officially closed on Sundays. But you don't run an office catering to fifty-seven types of refugees and five sources of funds without getting behind in paperwork. Maybe I can make a dent in the next four hours.

Maryam Yusuf (Mary to her face) is standing by the door. Forget paperwork.

"I've been waiting for hours."

"Sorry." I open the door. She goes in and sits down, carefully, and starts talking. I half listen. When I saw the black eye, I knew the story. Fourteen years old, adapting easily to Mann High School, turning from scared Iraqi-Assyrian refugee to American teenager, wears jeans/smokes/has a boyfriend/mouths off once too often. Her father, even a good guy like Sargon Yusuf, beats her up.

I'm sympathetic but not too much. She's bright and pretty but I don't sleep with my clients, especially the young ones. All these girls seem to know I'm divorced. And too many Maryams—Vietnamese, Khmer, Latino, Russian-Jewish, Assyrian, Haitian—have found in America the freedom to be addicts, whores, or criminals. Mary rambles on. When she mentions getting a knife for the future, I start shouting. Jake Abrams, in his worn gray suit with a knife in his shirt, overrides my cool.

That was the afternoon. No point in calling the social service agencies as I'm supposed to. Child-abuse paperwork is forever. And in crisis Sargon Yusuf forgets his English. I'd still have to translate.

I reach Sargon at the grocery store. It's Dad's yahrzeit, and Dad once owned that store. He cries about his wonderful daughter who left and yells at his disobedient daughter at the same time, stopping only to take care of customers as they walk in. I understand about half his Aramaic—I guess learning Talmud was

151

worthwhile. He slowly winds down. Maryam would be safe enough at home but tonight she'll stay at a friend's. Make sure the name is J-E-A-N and not G-E-N-E. Tomorrow, she and her parents will come in to talk. I know the speech I'll make by heart.

Four-fifty P.M., I'm late for shul. As I walk up the outside stairs, I hear a conversation. When I walk in, it suddenly stops. I guess I know the subject, especially as Dale looks flushed and angry. Dale makes a production of pointing toward Mr. Greenberg to indicate that I should be asked to lead minkha. It's a nice vote of confidence but I decline in Dale's favor. Bernie sits alone to a side, looking at his nine suspects. After a while, Joe Greenberg goes over to him. The words that reach me indicate that the two men belong to the same bowling league. None of the other detectives are here.

The minkha service is short, about ten minutes. As Dale repeats the standing prayer, I realize how much I need votes of confidence. Bernie is right. I am the logical suspect. Neither at the university nor at the League for Refugees do I have tenure. It's fall, but I'd better get this over before spring.

As Dale and I finish saying kaddish, the door to the building opens. Mrs. Abrams, looking composed, walks in and stands in the corridor. She hesitates, goes to the door of the shul and looks. All her life, she's been waiting for men in shul.

"Mike, why don't you say the mishnayos in honor of Dad?" I'm too tired to argue with Dale. Besides,

152

he's on my side. No one else in the shul really wants to hear mishnayos, especially not with me as the speaker, but they slowly assemble.

Bernie, however, is walking out. At first, I think he's just trying to avoid sitting through a boring interlude. But it's not that. Mrs. Abrams has caught his eye. She is pointing toward the coat rack. Of course, she's a first-generation immigrant woman who saves everything. She wants to take the coat back home.

My interest in an eighteen-hundred-year-old law code has suddenly vanished. I remember why I'm here. Jake Abrams, the knife, Maryam, the coat, Mrs. Abrams. I almost bump into Bernie.

"Excuse me, Bernie." But I don't get out of the way.

"Yeah. Now let me through. Mrs. Abrams wants to talk to me. I'll be back for the kaddish at the end of the mishnayos."

"No. You need to talk to me first. I know who the killer is."

Bernie sighs but is silent. Mrs. Abrams continues to wait. Dale and the others are assembling together for the mishnayos at the shul's other side.

"When was Mr. Abrams killed? It couldn't have been after he left here. There was no one in the basement."

"Except you. And few corpses walk out of a room and down a flight of steps."

"But did he? All I saw, all that anyone saw was a coat with a hood. You couldn't see the head, you couldn't see the feet of the person wearing it."

153

"Mike, we're ready to start." Bernie waves them to silence. To me, he says, "It was his coat."

"Exactly. He wore it in shul because he was always so cold. He walks out to take a piss, from the almost warm shul to the cold toilet, and he takes it off. And he doesn't leave it on a seat; it's neatly hung up on a coat rack."

"What was her motive?" Bernie hadn't been dumb in the old days, either. He's looking intently at the figure in the corridor as he whispers.

"Twenty-five years ago, Jake Abrams slapped us around. He stopped doing so. We got to be too big for him. Did he change? Did he stop being so free with his hands?"

"No, he didn't change." I talk too loudly. I'm more stunned by Mrs. Abrams walking into the men's area of the shul than by anything else that she has done. She still looks composed.

"Forty years of it. He hit me again last night. He could no longer drive; he went to the bathroom every ten minutes; but he could still hit. I drove him here this morning. He went downstairs to the bathroom. I went downstairs to find last week's paper. He said something. I saw the knife. . . ."

"Mrs. Abrams, I have to warn you that anything you say . . ."

Bernie could have saved his speech. Mrs. Abrams went on talking through it.

"Then I didn't know what to do. Until the body was found, I would be safe. I took the coat off him and

154

went upstairs. It hid me. Only then . . . I realized that there was going to be an exact minyan. If I could have been one of nine or of eleven, I could have done it. But not one of ten."

She shakes her head and walks out. Bernie follows her. Dale and seven others are waiting for me.

Murder, though it has no tongue...

MAURADE GLENNON

Maurade Glennon's first short story, "From Dublin's Fair City," won first prize in the 1964 Mademoiselle *magazine short-story contest; her second story received honorable mention in* Best American Short Stories. *Her first novel,* No More Septembers (1968), *was an alternate selection of the* Book of the Month Club; *her second,* The Waiting Time (1972), *won the Texas Writers Roundup novel award. She was born in Ireland and educated there and in the United States.*

DID SOMEBODY WHISPER in his ear, *I'm going to kill you,* or was he waking from a nightmare? He thought if he could concentrate he might identify the voice, but he was unable to make the effort.

He opened his eyes. He was alone in an unfamiliar white room that smelled of cleansers and disinfectants.

156

He tried to call out, *Where am I? How did I get here?* But no words came.

Panic took hold of him, mounted as he groped for a clue to his surroundings and almost went out of control when he had to ask himself, *Who am I?*

He was trying to calm himself when he heard an amplified announcement in a foreign language. His first thought was, *I've got to get out of here.* But when he tried to sit up a new horror gripped him: he could not move. Without having to think, he knew the right side of his body was the good one. The left side had been crippled ten years ago in a head-on collision that killed Bob, his only child.

So, he was not an entire blank. He had three memories: a collision, an impaired left side, a dead son.

He would think about all that later. Now he must explore his right side. He concentrated, straining with effort, until finger by finger, and toe by toe, he discovered he was locked up in a paralyzed body.

Though not completely. He could blink. He could swallow. He did both repeatedly while he was awake. And before he fell asleep he started trying to construct his past from two facts: he'd *had* a son; ten years ago he'd totaled a car.

He was wakened by a man's voice calling, "Señor! Can you hear me, Señor Simpson?"

Simpson. His relief was so great it took a few minutes to realize he knew the voice. Simpson, he thought, I am Jay Simpson. Before the accident I used to play the piano. I teach music appreciation. I live in . . . Where do I live? Austin! Austin, Texas. I spend part

157

of every summer in Mexico City. The last thing I remember is the splash of the fountain on Señora Valdez's patio outside my bedroom window. I am in Mexico City.

Jay opened his eyes. Dr. Alvarez, a near neighbor of Señora Valdez and one of her many cousins, was standing at the foot of his bed.

"If you understand me, señor, shut your eyes," the doctor said. "*Entiende?*"

Jay shut his eyes and didn't open them again till the doctor told him to do so.

"*Bueno, bueno,*" Dr. Alvarez said, and a tiny nurse, who had come to stand beside him, smiled with a great flash of white teeth. "You had a stroke . . ."

A stroke. But, Jay wanted to say, I always take my blood-pressure capsules and my diuretics. I exercise; I follow my diet; I avoid salt faithfully.

"The right side of your body is affected . . ."

I know, Jay thought, the good side.

"You are improving," the doctor assured him. "You have improved. And, of course, you are not alone. The señora, your wife, comes here every morning after she coaches her English-language students. She is already in the hospital. She will be with you soon."

The señora, his wife. Jay couldn't bring a wife to mind until she entered the room, asking, in English, "Is he conscious this morning, Doctor? Can he hear us?"

I can hear, Jay thought, swallow, see, remember. He was relishing those abilities with intense swamping

158

gratitude when his wife walked into his line of vision. A pink, scrawny woman wearing an unflattering, scoop-necked blouse and a red gathered skirt.

He knew, he *remembered* that this was the type of attire she always wore in Mexico and now referred to as "ethnic." Before that, the word had been "peasant," before that, "native." Her name, too, had gone through an evolution: Johanna to Joanne, to Joan, to Joni. A response, Jay supposed, to the fads of high school students to whom she had been teaching Spanish for fifteen years.

Joni walked to Jay's side, stripping teeth and gums in a wide grin, bent and put her lips against his ear and whispered, "I'm goin' to kill you, and that's a promise. But, sugar, keep rememberin' it's our secret."

Jay felt his heart skip a beat and pound two or three times. He raised his eyes in mute appeal to the doctor and the nurse, but both were casting indulgent glances at the touching embrace of husband and wife.

When Joni asked, "When can I take him out of hospital?" Jay again felt an uncomfortable action around his heart, and when the doctor shook his head, and the nurse frowned, he experienced an emotion close to love for both of them.

"It's too soon to talk about that, señora. Certainly not while we are dealing with enemas and a catheter."

Oh, blessed enemas, and twice-blessed catheter, protectors from promised murder!

Dr. Alvarez came around the bed to take Jay's blood pressure, and it was during that procedure that Jay thought of testing the fingers of his left hand. Had Joni told the doctor that though the accident had ruined his thumb and left him with an unbending wrist, he had never lost the use of his four fingers?

He waited till the doctor lifted his hand, and then, against the doctor's arm, he raised and lowered each finger.

Dr. Alvarez smiled. *"Bueno, señor. Muy bueno."* He moved each of Jay's fingers separately, and asked, "What would you do with a pencil, I wonder?"

"Nothing," Joni said. "The knuckles won't bend. There's no strength between the fingers."

"Claro, I see. Now, *amigo,* remember what they do in the movies? Blink once for 'yes' and twice for 'no.' Tell me, do you miss your music? *Sí?* I thought so."

Dr. Alvarez spoke to the nurse in rapid Spanish, and she left the room. Jay could not make the effort to understand what was said, but Joni assured the doctor he was *"muy simpático."*

When the nurse came back carrying a cassette player, Dr. Alvarez said, "You are in luck, *amigo.* My wife listens every night to this tape of our son, but yesterday when she left to visit her mother in Guadalajara, the 'rewind' control was stuck. By some miracle it was repaired in one day, so you'll have music, my son Jorge's music, till my wife returns."

Placing the cassette player under Jay's extended fingers, the doctor said, "Now, *amigo,* your first lesson. You will not, please, touch over here by the small finger. First, here is 'erase' control, which you will

160

never touch. Beside it, here, is 'record' control. You will not use it, please. If you press the 'record' control, it will erase Jorge's music and record the voices in the room. Now, under your index finger, is 'play.' Press. Hard. More hard."

Jay tried, and pressed again and again, till finally the notes of a xylophone tinkled in the room.

"*Bueno, muy bueno.* Now, under your middle finger is 'stop,' and beside it, 'rewind.' That's all you need to know. Try to stop the music, señor."

Jay tried, pressing till his finger trembled while the boy's thin voice sang, "*. . . en la primavera . . . son los pajaritos . . .*" It seemed to take minutes, but finally Jay depressed the 'stop' control on the first syllable of the word "*muchos*" and the cowlike *moo* made the doctor, the nurse, and even Joni laugh.

"Now try 'rewind,' there, to the left, next finger. Ah, more quick that time. Your fingers and the machine are working. Play, señor, but do not erase."

Jay could not resist testing the power of his index finger, and Dr. Alvarez guided him in locating and managing volume control through the previously interrupted line, "*. . . de muchos colores me gustan a mí.*"

While the music played, Joni dug an avocado out of her Mexican straw bag and said, "I heeded your warnings about my candy and cookie lunches, Doctor."

"I am glad to hear it, señora. But shall we find you some lemon for your avocado? Or chili?"

"*Nada*, thank you. I even got used to salt-free food when Jay had to do it. It spoils the taste for me now."

161

"All the better for you, señora," the doctor assured her before he left.

Through the afternoon Jay tried to cut out Joni's chatter with the xylophone. But he couldn't. She talked, and he felt compelled to listen for the word 'murder.' He tried not to, but he was unable to stop himself.

The days that followed took on the same pattern: bed-bath, enema, doctor's visit, a new tape for the day's music, his nine pills, the physical therapist, the afternoon rain that told him it was four-thirty, Joni's daily promise of death. Never more than one promise a day; never at the same time of day.

There was no way he could keep himself from waiting for that promise from the moment she walked into the room every morning. After she spoke his eyes would plead with her and he would try to form his lips into the word, Why? But if she understood she ignored the question.

With practice Jay learned to deal with the cassette player like a touch typist with a typewriter, and though he never used them, he was able to locate the 'erase' and 'record' controls as easily as the 'play' and 'stop' controls that he pushed many times a day.

In time the catheter was removed. His pills were cut to six. His outlook began to improve and he almost knew contentment. But the irony that better health meant a speedier exit from the hospital to his death was never far from his mind.

One morning he heard Dr. Alvarez, in the doorway,

telling Joni, "It would be against my wishes, señora," and he relaxed. But the next day, when Joni followed the doctor out of the room, and returned to tell Jay that in two days an ambulance would take him to Señora Valdez's, he knew fear again, and, as he was lifted into the ambulance, despair.

But the warm plump face of Señora Valdez soothed him, her tearful welcome cushioned his fears. Tired from the ambulance ride, he slept, and after he awakened, Señora Valdez brought him a black Oaxacan pot of red geraniums. He lay picturing the fountain on the old brick patio outside his room, listening to it splashing water into its circle of blue floral tile.

In this cool, bright familiar room, the days became stretches of music punctuated by Joni's commands to her ten students on the patio: "Repeat! Again!" And their voices, speaking of "jellow birds" and "beeg appleys" brought to Jay's mind, not yellow birds and big apples, but mangoes sculpted into flower shapes, purple bougainvillea trailing over adobe walls, the red ribbon Señora Valdez had tied to her struggling avocado tree to guarantee it seven years of life.

He became accustomed to the señora cooing to her finches as she aired them daily behind a patch of begonias. But he could not become accustomed to the woman who promised him death administering enemas, washing his body, spoon-feeding him salted, pureed food to speed his death.

Her own food was unsalted, not as she had told Dr. Alvarez, because she didn't like salt, but because she

163

didn't notice whether food was cold, greasy, spiced, bland. The woman had no palate, and often devoured limp tacos and cold tamales while she was reminding Jay to think about her reason for murder. He always blinked twice to show he didn't know, but wanted to know the reason. She never seemed to notice.

Then, one afternoon while she was assembling lunch leftovers on a tray, she said, "You do realize I'll have to do it mid-July at the latest. No, make that a week earlier to give me time for the funeral and all that and get me back in Austin early enough to prepare my classes."

You're insane, Jay thought, but even the insane have their reason, so tell me why. She continued to talk, describing plans for her fall courses, and Jay turned up the music volume. Without haste or anger she pressed the 'stop' control, and that, like the promise of murder, became a daily lunchtime habit.

Some evenings, when Dr. Alvarez dropped in on his way home, Joni spoke of taking Jay back to Austin, and when the physical therapist was present she asked him for tips to ensure her husband's comfort during the plane ride.

The doctor never forgot to exchange one tape for another and was apologetic when Jay had heard the last of his supply and had to start a repetition. Jay didn't mind. When he got tired of Mexican music, he'd press the 'stop' control and let Vivaldi, or Ravel, or, if he was agitated, Mozart or Bach run through his mind.

And lately he often lay in silence because he was suffering from blinding headaches and blurred vision.

He diagnosed a climb in his blood pressure and hoped the doctor would order him back to hospital. What the doctor did was change his medicine and increase his own visits to every other day.

The afternoon Joni picked up his new capsules she said, "You might as well see what I've been doing since, oh, for a long time now." Looking up at him, she added, "You surely didn't think I'd let you get away with killing my son, did you?"

So that was it; revenge for Bob's death.

"I'm real good at this," she explained, taking the capsule apart, emptying the powder into the bag from the *farmacia*, putting the capsule back together filled with salt. "I do believe I broke one. Hardly ever do that anymore, not after all the practice I've had. It doesn't matter now. You won't be around to finish this batch. See, I'll save all this powder and put it in your food one time. Or use what I've saved from other prescriptions." She took two old glass aspirin bottles out of her straw bag, showed him their powdered contents, then dropped them in the *farmacia* bag on top of the loose contents of his new capsules. Watching her empty more capsules into the bag, rather than into a bottle, Jay thought she was getting careless and inefficient, and he took some comfort from that thought.

"The time is perfect," Joni said. "Your friend, Dr. Alvarez, won't suspect a thing. Now, open your mouth."

To the best of his ability Jay clamped his mouth

165

shut. She forced his lips apart, pushed the capsule between his teeth and jaws, and kept his mouth shut till he gagged on salt. "Now, see? It can be nasty like that, or you can take it nice and easy. Or don't take it. It won't matter; you're still not getting your medicine. And I can put as much salt as I like in your food."

That evening he opened his mouth for the capsule and bit down as hard as he could on her finger. He meant it to be no more than a statement of his ability to fight back, but it angered her. She raised her hand to slap him, but arrested the movement, saying, "I must remind myself not to mark you up. You broke the skin, you maniac."

That evening the doctor noticed the band-aid on her finger, and she surprised Jay by saying "He bit me. When I was giving him his capsule."

Dr. Alvarez leaned over Jay and asked, "Mr. Simpson, are you refusing to take your medicine?"

Jay blinked once.

"Is it difficult to swallow?"

Two blinks.

"Then I wonder why." He took Jay's hand and said, "Amigo, I believe you are trying to tell us something. Am I correct?"

One blink, and the strongest pressure of fingers he could manage against the doctor's hand. Was he conveying anything? How much was Joni picking up?

Dr. Alvarez went to wash his hands in the tiny bathroom off their bedroom. "I will give him his medicine. It is here, is it not?" he called. "Don't bother," he added as Joni started toward him, then added, "What is this, señora? Salt?"

"Yes, for me. The señora cooks salt-free for Jay, so I add my own."

Did Jay imagine a pause during which he hoped Dr. Alvarez was recalling Joni's declining salt for her avocado at the hospital? Or was the doctor's "*Claro*," delayed simply because he was selecting the right medication from the assortment in the bathroom?

When the doctor went to Jay's bedside, Joni poured a glass of water from the bottle on the nightstand and handed it to him. The doctor asked, "Will you take this from me, *amigo*?"

Jay blinked twice and made frantic finger motions.

Saying "Those fingers . . . I still wonder . . ." the doctor dropped the capsule into his breast pocket while he was taking out his pen. It might have been an unconscious act. Be suspicious, Alvarez, Jay willed, think!

"Now, Mr. Simpson. Try to hold this pen between your fingers. Only hold. No more."

Jay saw the tension drop out of Joni as the pen dropped from his fingers.

"Relax, *amigo*. Maybe your therapist can work to make that back-and-forth movement as strong as the up and down."

"If that could be done, surely it would have been done before? In Austin?"

"Perhaps it did not seem as essential while your *esposo* had the use of his other hand. We will give him some good therapy at the hospital. And who knows, Señor Simpson? Maybe soon you will be writing us messages."

Joni's "No" was too loud, her "No hospital!" too sharp.

"Señora, Señora, do not agitate yourself. I must go to your country in one week. To San Francisco. It will only be a short while. Six days."

"I can take care of him while you're gone. Haven't I been doing that?"

"But now he will not take his medicine for you, señora. And even if I were staying, I would still put him back in hospital. We must do some tests. His blood pressure, señora. *Entiende?*"

The doctor took the capsules back to the bathroom, and while he was in there, Jay listened for and heard the rustle of paper. Maybe the doctor had opened the *farmacia* bag and seen its contents; maybe he had only moved the bag.

When Dr. Alvarez changed the tape in the cassette player, he said, "My son's tape again, señor. Guard it well!"

As soon as the doctor left, Joni said, "Well now, your *amigo* sure did speed up your death, didn't he? I couldn't risk another doctor, never mind tests, or you learning to write. Alvarez, I can fool; he'd never think of an autopsy. But I can't let you get to the hospital. Not at this stage. So that gives us a week. One week. And let me tell you, sugar, I do believe your fingers were strong enough to hold that pen."

Jay closed his eyes for fear they might reveal the truth of her suspicion, and kept them closed while she added, "I don't trust you one bit, not one little bit."

It encouraged him that she thought him formidable enough not to trust. And the one-week limit on his life sharpened his concentration; he searched desperately for some means of communicating with Dr. Alvarez. But what could he do? He had only his eyes, his teeth, the four fingers of his left hand; she had cunning, years of planning. Hatred. Salt. Poison.

During the night, in a flash of excitement, the answer came to him. Impatience kept him awake till daybreak, and after Joni woke up he kept closing his eyes for fear the light of hope might be shining out of them and visible to her.

When she left to join her students on the patio he was listening to Jorge singing *"De colores, de colores . . ."* And four hours later, carrying their lunch tray, she opened the door to the words, ". . . *se visten los campos . . ."*

While she was shutting the door with her foot, the tray rattled, and as it did, Jay pushed the volume control up fully. The sudden boom of the words, ". . . *los pajaritos que vienen de fuera . . ."* and the abrupt silence that followed threw Joni so off balance that the tray crashed to the floor.

"You maniac!" she screamed. "I'll destroy that tape!" She ran at him, mole sauce and guacamole salad streaming down her skirt. "I could strangle you!" she yelled, fingers clenched, arms extended. Abruptly she straightened up, gave a short laugh, and said, "That's why you did it. You *know* I'm going to kill you. You *know* you can't escape. You wanted to make me pay for your death. Well, let me tell you, I've put in too much time waiting for this chance to put in any more in a Mexican prison."

She left his side, and he heard her picking up broken pottery, dropping fragments on a metal tray. "I'll get that cassette player taken away from you," she muttered. "And let me tell you, the only reason I didn't destroy that tape was because it was made by that boy." She straightened up and said, "I believe I'll give you enough to kill you right now. And you can bite all you want; you can gag; you can choke on it for all I care. I'll have killed you one way or another. And you can't trick me into serving one day in prison."

She showered, dressed, forced three capsules down his throat, announced she was going out to get a complete list of flights to Austin. "For me," she explained. "You'll be buried in Mexico, to avoid complications." Before she left she said, "Now think of Bobbie when the pain starts."

Throughout the afternoon, anticipating pain, expecting death, Jay concluded his wife was now certifiably insane, but even allowing for that, could she ever have believed he had managed to rid himself of the wrenching guilt of having been the driver of the car that killed his son?

When she returned she said, "I lied. The capsules were empty. You didn't think I'd let you die without watching your pain, did you? I owe Bobbie more than that." She looked at her watch and said, "It's too close to the doctor's visit now, so you'll get a chance to live for the afternoon. I guess I'll do it soon after he leaves. Or maybe in the morning. We'll see."

Dr. Alvarez came later than usual, or so it seemed to Jay. "No music?" he asked. "You are tired of my son's xylophone? Truth to tell, *amigo*, I get a little tired of it myself, day after day. But you know mothers and their sons."

"Does he ever," Joni remarked, and Jay thought her control was slipping just a little.

She was standing beside his bed while she spoke, and Jay waited till she moved away to make room for the doctor before he pressed the 'play' control on the cassette player. The tinkling of the xylophone made Joni look around in surprise, and Jay met her eyes, and kept his gaze locked into hers while young Jorge Alvarez sang, "... *de colores se visten* ..." Joni looked at the doctor, then brought puzzled eyes back to Jay, and found his gaze still fixed on her.

"Blood pressure first, music later." As the doctor spoke he reached toward the cassette player, but Jay guarded the controls with his four good fingers, then increased the volume. The doctor continued to talk above his son's "... *de colores son los pajaritos* " and only stopped when Jay pushed the volume up fully, and again, exactly as it had happened that morning, the four words "... *que vienen de fuera* " boomed into the room. There was a moment of silence

171

before they heard the taped crash of the tray, the shattering of dishes, Joni shouting, "You maniac!"

After one look of disbelief she said, "He tricked me! He erased your son's music and he taped everything I said. Every word. I *knew* I couldn't trust him. I *said* I couldn't trust him. Did you hear me saying I was suspicious, Doctor?"

"I heard everything, señora."

It didn't occur to Jay to stop the tape, and as Joni talked he strained to listen to her two voices making different statements.

The doctor leaned over Jay and said, "I must persuade her to go with me when I phone the police. Will they find evidence? One blink, good. In the bathroom? *Sí.* Because I must tell you, señor, the capsule I took yesterday was empty. What would it prove? But you, Señor Simpson, are a very resourceful man."

Joni raised her voice above the volume of the cassette player and asked, "Doctor, do you realize he erased your son's tape? After you instructed him to be careful. What kind of man would do that? I couldn't do it, not to his mother. Please tell your wife that."

"Why don't you tell her yourself, señora? She's next door, visiting my cousin. And Señora Valdez will be glad to have you. You have a tray to return, do you not? I will carry it." While he was speaking he picked up the tray.

"Oh, well, Doctor, I'm not sure I want to . . ."

"But you understand mothers and sons, señora."

"Yes. Yes, I'll explain it to her, one mother to another."

172

Jay heard the patio door open and shut while the cassette player continued to emit Joni's voice saying "You know I'm going to kill you . . ."

Alone in the room he stopped the tape. Silence and peace settled around him.

Capriccio

ISAK ROMUN

"Capriccio" marks the second appearance of the Isak Romun byline in NBM. *This story resulted from the author's thoughts, while attending a concert, about the different performances of the same composition. A volume of Monahan stories is in the works.*

EVERYONE WAS CROWDED into the large room buttock on buttock, as if packed in by a Japanese train guard. Clumsy waitresses in short black dresses and white aprons maneuvered trays of drinks through the mass of squirming and unpredictable bodies, maybe spilling one drink for every two for which they found thirsts. Overhead, a chandelier threw down a fierce light as its teardrop baubles, moving with the rising heat, tinkled short, awkward messages to the drinkers below. Around the room, huge fabric panels showed Versailles garden scenes. I wondered what those unbathed and lice-ridden elegants, strolling in the gardens and looking down from the walls, thought of the crowd below them.

The room was a late renovation at the Paulsburg Academy for the Performing Arts and must have cost Karol Kinseca, the director, a tidy sum. But he probably got it all back from this one night's concert.

As I came in, the first face I recognized belonged to Erwin Jacoby, our paper's part-time music critic. He was a small man with dormouse features and a dusty pince-nez pinned on to them. Jacoby had a solid musical education. He could have done well in one of the big music centers but for a hypertensive condition that brought him to the quiet of Paulsburg. He owned a music store and appeared satisfied with his life in the provinces.

He spotted me and came over, plainly agitated and shaking an empty champagne glass in my direction. "She's crazy, you know. You hear what she's doing to Köchel 242 next season? Her old game."

"I'm dying to know," I said, familiar with Jacoby's passions, one of which was that no one, but no one, touches a note of the Mozart canon.

"She's doing a reduction for one piano. Says Mozart took a single part and parceled it out to three of his no-talent students. She says she's achieving Mozart's spiritual and aesthetic intent. Also, it costs a bundle to get three world-class pianists together."

"So?"

"So if Mozart wanted to transcribe the concerto's three solo parts for single piano, he would have done it."

"Maybe he wouldn't. Mozart the composer did damn little because he *wanted* to, mostly because he *had* to."

"Oho, now Monahan is the great music historian," Jacoby snorted and started stomping off to complain to someone else.

"Hold it," I said, grabbing him by a frayed sleeve. "Did you call in your review?"

"Of course."

"Well?"

"Well what?"

"Well, what did you say about the *Capriccio*?"

"What am I, the town crier? Read tomorrow's paper."

"Tell me now." I still held his sleeve and had no intention of letting go anytime soon.

Jacoby let out an exasperated breath. "I said Terence Scobie has at last arrived as a composer. He's come out of the woods. He's suddenly found the year he's living in. There are still discernible traces of derivative romanticism in the *Capriccio*, but Scobie has taken a giant step into the twentieth century with this work which, despite influences, stands as the capstone of his corpus. Cormain Scobie, his estranged wife (I didn't mention that), is today's foremost woman conductor. I went further and said she probably ranks among the top ten conductors in the world. Finally, I said she perfectly realized the *Capriccio*, that in her hands it was an exciting, riveting aural experience. Something else I didn't put in my review: It's pretty strange when the composer, at the great moment in his creative life, isn't on hand to take a bow."

"You know how Terence is about listening to his music live."

"I know, but I don't understand." Jacoby looked searchingly around the room. I figured he wanted something liquid. Maybe a lot of it. "Now, Monahan," he said, coming back to me, "is it okay if I refill this glass and find someone a little more interesting to talk to, like that pretty thing over there having trouble with her whalebone? Want more information, read the paper you work for. You get a free copy, cheap-skate."

"Thanks," I said, and took my hand from his sleeve.

"Thanks? I wouldn't write what I wrote if I didn't mean it."

"You are an upright man and are released. And watch the old blood pressure. Whalebone in disarray can have an arousing effect on aging music critics."

Jacoby, mumbling, went off in the general direction of one of the waitresses momentarily mired between a fat man in a thin man's suit and the "pretty thing" whose strapless gown seemed held up by antigravity but more likely by the press of bodies around her.

I felt a pressure on my elbow and turned to look into the tired and slightly red eyes of Terence Scobie. Terence always looked and acted as though he were wearing a smoking jacket—he had that secure and set-

177

tled look, though the appearance belied the character around which it was wrapped. Yet it was that serene image he projected to the world. Even now, in his mandatory tux, he seemed to belong in a study, brandy globe in hand, idly swishing the amber fluid while standing before a glowing (not roaring) fire.

Terence was a tidy, medium-sized man, whose dark hair, now nicely graying at the sides, was disposed evenly over his head and parted precisely in the middle. He wore glasses that seemed to draw those tired eyes out of his head so that they overhung a curiously undistinguished button nose. No matter how well you knew him, you never thought to call him Terry, though he invited the nickname.

He nodded toward Jacoby some feet away from us. "I gather you just got the news of Cormain's intended ravishment?"

"Ah yes, Jacoby's off and running. Guardian of the deposit of faith, that sort of thing. Particularly where Mozart's concerned."

Terence smiled slightly as, with some trouble, he guided me across the room toward a table in a corner. On it rested a large, almost square volume bound in cordovan leather with gold lettering on the cover. He picked up the book and handed it to me. "For you, Oscar," he said simply. "The manuscript of the score."

I looked at the cover and read the two lines there: "*Capriccio* for Orchestra, Opus 49, by Terence Scobie." I said, "You know I'm a musical illiterate. Sure you want to waste this on me?"

"For a variety of reasons I want you to have it. Open

178

it." I did so and saw the title page. "No, no," he said, "the next page."

On the next page, I read my name on the dedication. I made a low whooshing sound with my mouth and looked at Terence.

"Surprised? You're as much responsible for tonight as anyone."

"A few articles."

"And you went to New York and persuaded Cormain to come down here and do the premiere."

"That was pleasure."

He breathed in heavily, the way a man does who's going to unload something on you, and can't quite believe what he's going to say. "We'll announce it tonight. We're going to get married. Is that the correct term when you retie the knot with an ex-wife? Of course, *you* would say we've always been married, and anything we do now just satisfies the state and not"— he looked up at the domed ceiling, a continuation of the Versailles theme done in tasteful pastels—"the great Maestro in the sky."

"I don't care what you call it," I said, "I call it great." I'm afraid I'm an insensitive prig who believes that solemn vows, once exchanged, are binding.

"My cup runneth over even more. The *Capriccio* will be published, and RCA is talking about recording it with Cormain on the podium."

Just then I spotted a pretty black-haired woman across the room. She was wearing a low-cut white dress spangled with fake gems that caught the light and turned it into a thousand tiny rainbows. It was a dress

179

that might be smashing on a beautiful woman or on a homely woman, and that somehow seemed to sag and slip on merely pretty Viveka Hussey. I nodded in her direction and said, "Ah—" in a meaningful way.

"Viv will understand," Terence said.

I looked over at Viveka as she tried to control all that dazzling elegance in which she was smothering. I wasn't sure, considering the stakes, she had it in her to be understanding. When Terence and Cormain broke up, he kept up a front, but those of us who knew him—and I'd known him since we were kids—weren't fooled. He taught his classes at Paulsburg College as usual and taught them well, but there was a slacking-off of production. For one full year, he composed nothing, worked at nothing. Clearly, there was a vacuum to be filled, and Viveka, shortly after she joined the college music department, filled it. Terence started getting notes down on paper again, mostly key-board music because piano was what Viveka taught. Some of his music began finding its way to records, usually the smaller labels, the last a full program of his *Forest Etudes* and other piano pieces performed by Viveka in a *giutamente ma non brillante* style (to cite Jacoby's review of the time). Although the *Capriccio* was not a keyboard composition, she unquestionably provided the motivation that resulted in its composition. There was campus scuttlebutt that she was to become the second Mrs. Scobie.

Well, that was all out the window now.

"Where, by the way," I asked Terence, looking to

180

steer my mind in another direction, "is the eminent conductor?"

"Where would you think?" Terence said and gestured languidly toward a tight circle of men, among them Karol Kinseca and Carmen Burell, the Paulsburg Symphony's concertmaster. I wondered at these two in the circle, smiling and nodding ceremoniously, concealing with smooth, meaningless words what must have been smoldering inside. Cormain was a wonderful woman, but a hard one. I had heard that at rehearsals she remorselessly criticized Burell's bowing technique, his rapport with the music, and his understanding of music in general. You don't do that to a concertmaster, not in front of the orchestra with which he's associated. I understood he walked out of the last rehearsal. He came back for the concert, though.

In the case of Kinseca, he was a big talent situated improbably in Paulsburg. He had crossed barbs with Cormain over a matter of the placement of her name on some posters outside one of the nation's prestigious concert halls of which Kinseca was director at the time. The posters stayed—it was too late to print replacements—but Kinseca didn't. In a matter of days, he found himself traveling south, lucky to get the job in Paulsburg.

A chink developed in the circle, and I caught a glimpse of Cormain at its center.

She was not beautiful, she was not even pretty. Character rode a face in which mere good looks would have been a disfigurement. She wore a dress of severe design, black with a slash of off-white at the right shoulder. Her eyes moved slightly from one man to another in a way devised to make each believe her attention was his. Occasionally, she would raise a hand to cheek in false and graceful shock at something said.

I thought how well Viveka's dress would look on Cormain, a case of spirit conquering cut. To me Cormain was then as she had always been: controlled perfection. If she had a weakness, it was her belief that everyone should forgive her anything.

Just then she spotted me and called to Terence— she called him Terry, the only one I knew who did— to stop holding me prisoner.

"Go ahead," Terence said, giving me a slight push in the direction of Cormain. "I have to hear the *Capriccio*. Just before you came in, they told me they had the tape set up."

"You haven't heard it yet?"

"No, and please no discourse on my strangeness. I get enough of those from Jacoby and others."

He waved wanly to Cormain, gave me another push, then turned and made his way from the room.

I went over and joined the gallery of men around Cormain.

As parties go, I suppose this one was a success. All the booze was gone and the *hors d'oeuvres* still around were soggy and inedible if they hadn't been before. The room looked as if an artillery battery had performed a time-on-target barrage on it. The guests, for the most part, were gone, but not before Karol Kinseca got to each one and extracted a pledge for the Academy.

Kinseca was among the few people left. Terence, Carmen Burell, and Viveka Hussey were there, too, as was the working press represented by Erwin Jacoby (I was a guest). A few other people milled around hoping Kinseca would break out a fresh supply of liquor. (Fat chance! He already had their signatures on pledge cards.) Cormain had left to "powder her nose" in her dressing room.

Earlier, Cormain had made the announcement of Terence's and her upcoming wedding, followed by the good news that the *Capriccio* not only would be published but recorded as well. Each of these announcements was commemorated by fresh toasts among the near-insensible guests, some of whom, in a delirium of joy, passed out and had to be carried from the room to waiting limousines below.

Yes, it was a thoroughly successful party, but I thought it time for me to go home. It had been a busy night and I was exhausted. Besides, although I had made her promise not to do it, I knew my sister Maureen was waiting up for me. So, with Terence's score under my arm, I got ready to take off.

But when I went to say good-bye to Terence, he said, "No, you can't go, Oscar. Cormain and I want you to have late supper with us at the Jefferson. Just the three of us."

"How about a rain check?"

He shook his head. "Tonight only happens once."

"Then spend it with your wife—or wife-to-be. Whatever."

Again he shook his head.

"Okay, then, but where is she? A hundred noses could be powdered in the time she's been at hers."

"She's probably changing. Let's speed her up."

We went out of the party room. The Academy was dark this time of night. All the rank-and-file musicians had long ago left, and the technicians, lights out and gear stowed away, had gone home, too. In the corridor, Terence and I found our way lit by a series of half-power lamps, spaced far apart, which challenged the dark and came up losing. We went down this corridor and through a door to as dimly lit a stairwell, descended the stairs and came out on the floor that was level with the stage. The dressing rooms were on this floor. We guided ourselves, hands on walls, along another corridor past several doors until we came to one with Cormain Scobie's name on it. A straight edge of light stretched across the width of the door at bottom. "Well, at least she's home," Terence said. "Knock, Oscar."

I did, and got no answer. I knocked again and called her name. Still no answer. I said, "Maybe she's not at home after all."

"She's probably dozing. Knock louder."

I did. Nothing.

"Try the knob."

I turned the knob and the door swung in. Before I

184

had a chance to look into the room, Terence, who was behind me, said in one of those whispers that has the unnerving intensity of a scream, "Oh my God, my God!"

When he said this, I turned, just in time to catch him. He was out. I eased him to a position against the wall. Then I went to the dressing-room door and pushed it wide. Cormain *was* "at home."

I had two bodies on my hands: one in a dead faint, the other dead.

I was in Cormain's dressing room. Her body had been taken away. I was glad, for even with a sheet covering the lifeless form I could imagine the face swathed in blood that had escaped from the deep gouge in the skull plate above. The murder weapon had been taken too, a slim crystal flower vase with an etched network of willow leaves over it. There were no surfaces large enough to capture a fingerprint and, though the police dusted the piece, they had no hope of lifting anything off it. They didn't.

They checked for prints elsewhere and found everyone's in the room, including mine. They also found mine on the doorknob, naturally.

This last fact was something the large man with me in the dressing room went to a lot of trouble to point out. "So, Monahan," he said, "come clean. Why did you kill her?"

"Actually, we were both in contention for the Boston Symphony podium, and I thought with her out of the way—" I stopped and reviewed in my mind what I had said. "Why am I going along with the joke? It's not funny, Heck."

Lieutenant Hector Aloysius Brosnan, Paulsburg Police Department, sighed. It was like a train going through a tunnel. "No, it's not, Monahan. But if I couldn't push a little laugh into this thing every so often, I'd have to quit this line of work and switch over to helping the meter maids."

"Who'll it be?" I asked. "Besides me, that is. Damn, I can't drop it."

"Take your pick," Brosnan answered. "All the ones with strong motives snuck down here to talk with her about one thing or another. We found this out upstairs during our preliminary questioning. All except Kinseca and your friend Jacoby, or so they say. But either one could have come down, too. No one would notice a person sneaking—"

I interrupted. "You don't seriously believe Erwin Jacoby would have done it? He hardly knows—knew —Cormain Scobie."

"But he was plenty irritated at her tonight for something. Changing somebody's music."

"Mozart's. Who's been dead for over one hundred and seventy-five years. If he got angry, it's his critical reflex. It doesn't amount to anything."

"Maybe. Anyway, as I was saying, anyone could have come down here. Everyone was in and out of that room where the party was. Some to go to the head, some to sneak down here and see her."

"I guess I know why two of them came down—and

186

why Kinseca didn't. Viveka Hussey wanted to tell Cormain to leave town the way she came: without Terence Scobie. Burell probably wanted Cormain to do something to restore his prestige with the orchestra."

"Write a letter. A kind of thick thank-you, what in the Army we used to call a letter of commendation. And she was going to do it—according to Burell. Your guess on the Hussey woman is on target. That leaves Kinseca and Scobie."

"Terence Scobie," I said tonelessly. "He's just had the triumph of his life. His work is going to get published. Be recorded. He reunited with his wife." I stopped a moment. Then, in the same flat voice, asked, "Why in heaven's name would he do it?"

"I never said he was high on my list, Monahan. Just as you're not high on it. Lucky you. What about Kinseca?"

"He wouldn't have had to see her. It wouldn't have done any good. Even if Cormain was sorry for shafting him, there was nothing she could do about it. It's easier to push someone out of a job than in. Besides, Karol seems happy down here, and he's not the vengeful sort. He's really poured himself into the Academy."

"Yeah, but I think his wallet would be lumpier back where he was. I was born in Paulsburg, but have no illusions about it. We're in the sticks, laddy."

It must have been after eleven when Terence and I found Cormain's body. I called the police from a wall phone outside the dressing room and, in minutes, Brosnan and his crew were there. They sealed off the Academy shortly after we got back upstairs to tell the

187

others what happened. It was now after one in the morning and I knew I was knocked out. Brosnan, who I knew had been roused out of his house by the homicide call, couldn't have been any more rested than I. Yet he looked fresh, as if he could go on for hours yet. It was probably no more than a nervous response to the task before him; but, nervous or not, I was afraid he might carry me along with him.

I nodded upward. I asked, "Going to let them go? It *is* late."

"Why not?" he said. "I know which one it is, anyway."

"Are you going to share this piece of special information with me?"

"With a newsman? You're a darling man, Monahan, but no way!"

"Just a few minutes ago you were asking questions. Now you know who it is. How'd this happen?"

He poked an index finger, thick as a sausage, against his temple. "Zee little green cells, m'sieur."

"They're gray, and I've heard that line before. Going upstairs now and read him or her his or her rights?"

"If you're Irish, they're green." He brought the finger down to his chin and massaged the stubble there. "I have a few things to put together and then I pounce. Come on up with me. I'm going to let you all go home. Give the killer a false sense of security and, then, the knock in the night. Nervous, Monahan?"

I didn't answer. There had been enough jokes.

We left to go upstairs to the others. I was down the

corridor some distance before I remembered that I had put Terence's score on a table in the dressing room. I went back and got it.

Yet, tired as I was, I didn't go home. There was too much trying to worm its way into my mind. I was exhausted into wide-awakeness. I drove my car around town, guiding it through streets and up alleys that were not my choices. Occasionally, I would seem to come alive and become vaguely conscious of what I was doing. I would look around me with curiosity and alarm, unable to put together that which, in the light, would be the parts of familiarity. I could have been driving my car through fog, for all the recognition of where I was and where I was going was concerned.

Nonetheless, I have a faded-gray memory of approaching lights, of cars passing me, some of them police cruisers. None of the drivers paid any attention to me. I wasn't drunk, but I was driving like a drunk under control, not slow but on the underside of the speed limit, staid and straight, not daring to let tire tread wander over yellow line. I wasn't thinking and yet I knew I was waiting for thought. I was ready. No, wrong word; I was receptive. My senses had telescoped up and out from my body, tensing, waiting for me to pick up the message I knew was out there. It was waiting for me to drive to the place or to the time in which it would become clarity.

It wasn't to come right away. I pulled into a super-market parking lot and stopped the car. I wanted to call my sister and tell her I was all right. I turned the engine off, but before I could put the keys in my pocket, sleep caught up with me. I fell over with my hand clenched around the keys. It was a dreamless sleep, the kind I don't mind having and the kind I hate to come out of.

The next thing I remember was my name, repeated over and over, faintly, as if the sound were emerging from water. I came around and saw a ball of light above the car reflected in what seemed to be a rectangular pool of blood. "Mr. Monahan!" It was sharper now, nearer, and perhaps held as much anger as concern.

I had slumped over. I pulled myself to a sitting position and looked through the windshield and the rear window and the glass at the passenger side. All the wrong places. "Monahan!" Extremely sharp this time, irritated without doubt. I looked through the window at my left shoulder and saw there a face I thought could only have been dredged up into life by the dark itself.

And then its features became not at all frightening, work-weary and exasperated, perhaps, but not frightening. It was a cop I knew. I looked beyond him and saw his motorcycle. The ball of light became a parking-lot lamp, the pool of blood its reflection on the cover of Terence's score. I rolled down the window.

"Mr. Monahan, you all right?" the face asked. "Your sister called into the station downtown. Under the influence? Can I get someone to take you home?"

"I'm all right, Boycie, and I'm not drunk," I replied with dignity. "And I don't wish to go home. I have a phone call to make." I looked momentarily down at the score resting on the seat. Then I looked back at the policeman. "Two calls, for that matter. Do you have any idea where I can find a phone?"

Boycie waved toward a bank of lighted telephone booths hugging the outside wall of the supermarket. He said, "Monahan, go home!" then got on his motorcycle and left me alone in the lot. I got out of my car and walked over to one of the booths.

I got in the booth and searched my pockets for a coin. I had none. That settles it, I thought, I'm not supposed to call anyone. Forget it. Monahan, go home!

Absently, a habit trailing back to childhood, one of my fingers searched the coin-return receptacle. I felt a thin dime at its smooth and slippery bottom. I pulled up the coin against the curved surface of the receptacle, and, coin secured between thumb and index finger, lifted it to the slot at the top of the phone. I let the dime clink down and into the metallic insides of the phone. Then I dialed the operator.

When she came on I put in a collect call to my home. Maureen answered, and after she got through lecturing me on how expensive collect calls were and didn't I have a dime? I told her I was okay and to stop putting the Paulsburg police on my trail.

"When will you be home?" she asked.

"I probably won't. So just stop worrying. I'm a big boy."

191

I hung up and fished around in the change return for the dime that had dropped there when I placed the collect call. I put the dime back into the phone and dialed a number. After several rings, Jacoby answered.

"I want to come over and see you," I said into the receiver. He said something. I checked my watch. "So it's after three." He almost hung up, and I said quickly, "I could bring Brosnan, but I just want to talk to you alone." I waited while he asked what the hell he had to do with Brosnan. After some more argument and explanation, he said grudgingly, "Okay, come over!" I hung up and went back to my car, started it up, and drove to Jacoby's place.

I rang the bell. A voice commanded, "Come in!" I went in.

He was at a desk in his living room. Only a single light was on, a desk lamp that threw a circle of white light on the desktop and, through its glass shade, a soft, green color that fell into the lines of his face and made him look coarse and unfamiliar. He had been writing. Now he folded the sheet of gray paper he'd been writing on, placed it carefully in a gray envelope, sealed the envelope, wrote on its face, and turned it, writing down, on the desk. He looked up at me.

"You brought the score," he said.

"I've had it with me all night."

"You haven't been home?"

I shook my head.

"You've thought it out then?"

I nodded slowly. "With some help. I've just come from Erwin Jacoby's."

"I wouldn't think you'd need help, Oscar."

"Jacoby says I'm okay, but only a well-tempered listener." I tapped the leather cover of the volume I held at my side. "He went over this with me. After he did, he said you still have eyes in the back of your head."

"The better to look back to the nineteenth century, eh?" He stared up at me, started to stand up, then sagged back into the chair. "At the tape session, I heard my *Capriccio* for the first time." He shifted irritatedly in the chair. "I might have known if she wouldn't spare Mozart, she certainly would have no mercy on me, a middling talent stuck away on an unknown campus. She said that to me. Will you believe that?"

"Personally, what tears me up, Terence, is that you used me to lend credence to what you planned to tell the cops. That great fainting scene. Of course, you expected me to tell them about that. 'So distraught at the sight of his dead wife, Officer—' And you let me discover her!"

"To put your mind at rest—at least a little bit—on one point. I did pass out."

"That doesn't matter. If you hadn't, you would have faked it."

"Oscar, an artist will defend that which he creates, even if he doesn't like it, over that which he loves. Sure, my notes were all there, but so were a number of hers. And the markings, the tempi, the emphases were

193

distorted. In places, my adagios became andantes; my andantes, allegros; my allegros, vivaces. And, Oscar, they liked it!"

"If they hadn't, she might be alive now, having supper with us, telling us how wrong-headed she'd been."

He got up from the chair, paced across the room, entering its portions of darkness, returning to the light. He sat down again.

I said, "You've got to pay, Terence. No collection of notes is worth a life." I remembered her, the blood.

He smiled. "You might say, face the music, eh?"

"If you want to be cute about it."

"She killed me."

"You've got to pay."

"I suppose so." He picked the gray envelope off the desk. "Here," he said resignedly, "deliver this to your Lieutenant Brosnan."

I took the envelope. "Good-bye," I said.

"Good-bye, Oscar," he answered. "Don't lose that score. Maybe someday you can get it performed."

He walked to the door with me, which I thought was a strained courtesy considering the circumstances. As I turned in the doorframe, he said, "It was clever, working all that out."

"Not really. I've known all night you killed her. I just didn't know why. That's what I was doing, driving all over Paulsburg looking for the why."

He laughed. It was a small laugh, deep in his throat. "All night, you say? You've known all night?"

"At her dressing room. When I started to open the

194

door, you passed out. But I hadn't opened it all the way, and you were in back of me. You couldn't see her; neither could I. Your memory delivered the image your eyes couldn't."

The sun was breaking the horizon as I walked toward the entrance of police headquarters. The light was split by the steeple of St. Francis Xavier, three blocks eastward. The steeple threw across my path two bars of light separated by a band of darkness. As I went up the headquarters steps, the church bells began ringing. I thought of my sister Maureen, probably sitting stiffly in a pew, awaiting the start of early Mass.

It was around six, and no one was wide awake enough to take much notice of me in the headquarters building. Besides, I was known there. I went up to the second floor to Brosnan's office. I wasn't surprised to find him at his desk.

Before I could say anything, he announced, "We just got word, one of our patrols. Scobie's dead. Shot himself. A neighbor heard the shot."

I hadn't expected that, and perhaps should have. But it was no surprise. It was all according to some baleful logic. Scobie, despite his apparent control, was a romantic in more than his music. I said to Brosnan, "I've just come from there," and gave him the envelope.

He opened it carefully, took out the gray paper inside. It couldn't have been a long note. It was only a small piece of paper written on one side. I'm sure Brosnan read it more than once, he kept it that long.

"I never figured this," he said, offering me the note. I waved it away. "Why?" he asked.

I told him why.

"For a piece of his music?"

"For a piece of his soul."

Brosnan shook his head slowly as he replaced the note in its envelope.

"Do you mind telling me who you were going to put the finger on?" I asked.

"Yes, I do mind, Monahan. The police can't share all their information with the press. Particularly when some of that information is bad. I've got to get over there. Want to come?"

"I'm going to bed."

I walked Brosnan down to his car parked at the curb outside the headquarters building. "Sure you won't come?" he asked. I said no. He got in and drove off.

I stood for a while on the pavement. I was facing so that Francis Xavier's steeple dominated my vision. I started walking toward the church. I remember thinking that, later on, Father Bax, in his gentle way, would probably chew me out for coming in after the Gospel.

You Can't Fire Me for Doing My Job

CLARK DIMOND

Clark Dimond is a novelist, comic-story writer, and magazine editor. He is the author of No-Frills Mystery, *the generic novel published by Jove in 1981, and he has written stories for* Creepy *and* Eerie. *Mr. Dimond has edited* True Experience *and* For Men Only *magazines, and he is currently editing and publishing* Brunt, *a humor magazine. "You Can't Fire Me for Doing My Job," a detective story without a crime, was drawn from his experiences as a private investigator in New Jersey.*

THOUGH I'VE BEEN CALLED worse, I'm just an independent dick.

I've been in the business for a while. Worked my way up from agency security and guard duty. Up is the only way to go from there.

It's a job. For a job not to eat your stomach up, you need a hobby. I like to think about fitting things together.

197

Some things seem to fit together naturally. I just know there was joy in the heart of the first guy who figured, probably by association and trial, that the large section of a car antenna is .22 caliber, leading to the discovery of the zip gun.

I am a hobbyist of sorts, and I don't like to go around unarmed. I like to have a surprise ready just in case I need a backup. When the boss wanted his gun returned, I needed something to make up for the security I lost, and the cosh I carried wasn't long enough to keep me totally out of reach of the average large thief.

Funny thing. A store dick's not a regular employee of the store he prowls for boosters, but of the security agency. I had to cross employee picket lines in the line of work. There was a civil-rights boycott of certain dime-store lunch counters. So I got pretty restless and I was young. My life stretched out before me in the land that held for me no promise of compromise.

I complained to my boss, the ex-cop running the local dick franchise, who explained, while promoting me to nighttime security guard in Brickville, that I wouldn't have trouble with picketers there. "People don't picket stores that ain't open yet."

"I don't mind night work," I said. "After all, the only boosters I catch are kids. . . . Oh, and that lady who wore her hat and suit and shoes out the door with the price tags still dangling. And hell, I was tempted to boost a pair of gloves the other day myself."

"This is a uniform job. On this one you're *supposed* to look like a cop."

"I have a friend with a P-38 Walther I might borrow."

"You'll look like the Gestapo. And besides, they jam, those automatics. Use a revolver. Use mine with the Sam Browne belt."

"What do I do?"

"Make three rounds an hour. Look, I'll meet you down there at six. Show you around the place."

"What'll I be protecting?"

"Mostly copper tubing."

"All night every night?"

"Yeah. But if you don't work out as a night guard, we can put you on for a couple of hours a day at the Mall taking candy from babies."

"Sounds like fun."

"Can't eat on the floor of the discount house at the Mall."

"I get the picture," I said. "Young suburban mom in white pinafore buys a lollipop for her little Wally, a drooler. Flies are sticking to the slobber-eroded valleys that have already formed on his downy cheeks; but for the moment, to Mom's satisfaction, he's not crying. No food at the discount house, so I take the huge twirly caramel stickum out of his grubby paws and plop it down in the ashtray sand. He starts to bawl. And she screams."

"If you've got an automatic, she'll scream Gestapo."

"A revolver keeps things cool?"

"You should never have to unbutton your holster."

"What if I have to draw it?"

"This isn't the Wild West, sonny. The draw is in

two motions. It gives fair warning of your intentions. You unbutton the holster, then you draw. My weapon is a double action with a hair trigger. It's always cocked. Don't drop it. Try not to fall down. There's always a bullet under the hammer. No empty cylinders. You getting this down?"

"Yes, sir. But I still want a job where I can wear a suit."

"I told you the first day. When you wear a suit you look like a cop. I told you. When you're working in the stores, wear grease in your hair. Look like the customer. Fade into the walls."

"Can't I blow-dry my hair now if I'm in uniform?"

"That's okay, but you'll always be wearing a hat. So what's the difference?"

"It'll make me feel better. . . ."

"Cleaner? This is not a clean job, kid."

And it wasn't. The copper tubing I was guarding down in Brickville was in a dusty construction site, but it was no great challenge. I could work four hours on store security and still make my rounds at night. I was guarding a roofless shell. There were loading pallets, holes, and trenches in the dirt, but no corners behind which a thief could hide for long.

My office was in the construction trailer, of course. The radio was always on. I could listen to Wheeling or Chicago until dawn, but in the cheery desk-lit trailer I found a tendency to rock back on the chair like a deputy in a Western, put my feet up on the desk, and sort of nod out for twenty minutes at a time.

I spent the first night taping my truncheon, a billy club made out of rough-textured iron with two steel spring sections that telescoped inside, which would pop out like a gravity knife when shaken with a twist of the wrist. I soldered a bolt at the tip end for added weight and after I had removed the useless pen-clip that couldn't support the truncheon's weight and tended to tear any pocket, I taped the rough texture of the iron with the sort of care I had previously reserved for baseball bats. The advantage of this sort of club was obvious. Each end had a different use. The light end was a coil-spring knuckle duster. With the soldered bolt instead of a plastic safety tip it was no longer harmless, since I filed it so it would cut. And whip-fast. The short butt end was a lethal cosh.

I found a length of iron sewer pipe that a tennis ball or beer can would just fit inside, and I found some dynamite fuse in the construction trailer. I figured I could punch a hole in a tennis ball and feed the fuse inside.

At night, thinking I might need reinforcement sometime, I mined the perimeter of the area I was guarding with a couple of black powder mortars. I welded a square plate to the base of the pipe. I drilled holes in a couple of tennis balls and funneled them full of 4FG powder—a much better grade than the homemade black. Then I ducoed a three-inch length of dynamite fuse into the holes and left the tennis balls sitting in the sewer pipe, into which I'd tapped fuse holes, like cannons have.

Ever since I fitted a 16-gauge shotgun shell into the pole of a beach umbrella and found that it fit, I had become obsessed with the pursuit of high-quality lawn furniture. I had cut a length of umbrella pipe, chambered spent shells from which I removed the pin-dented primer, and inserted dynamite fuse. It just fit.

It had been a matter of a few minutes to add these to my sewer pipe mortars and train them on the area I was guarding. On my rounds at night I strung fuse to my "wooden arsenal," my euphemism for toy guns since childhood.

Tired of weaponry as a full-time hobby after the third night, I brought a Gibson mandolin with a cracked neck, which I glued and clamped at the security desk. My mother bought it at a rummage sale. I practiced chords between my rounds.

The boss wanted his gun back a couple of days after that. As many as he owned, he seemed to need my loaner for some reason. I had spent my salary on uniforms but hadn't earned enough for any store-bought weapon but the cosh.

The trailer window that fronted my desk was high enough off the ground that only a basketball player on tiptoe could see if I was at the desk. There was a bathroom in the middle of the trailer, separating it into two rooms. The bathroom had two doors. About the time I was ready to make my rounds, I would open the desk-side door to the bathroom, sit on the john lid for several minutes to accustom my eyes to darkness, get my night vision, then move into the dark end of the trailer and past the silent magnetic-latched door into the night. I varied my moves. Sometimes I was the jaunty obvious stooge bumbler, sometimes the darkest commando to raid Calais.

On the ninth night I got some action.

I had done an obvious turn for my unseen and imaginary audience of thieves. Upon reentering the lighted door of the construction trailer I stood silhouetted in the doorway with an immense Macanudo cigar. I lit it and yawned, stretching excessively, as in a silent movie. I felt no undue risk in such a gesture. No one would resort to assassination of a guard in order to obtain copper tubing. With the sound of WWVA on the radio, if anybody was watching I would be presumed to be sitting somewhere in the office, relaxing with my midnight cigar. In fact, I had left it to go out in the ashtray. I slithered down the steps by the silent darkened door that faced away from the construction, wormed through a gap in the trailer skirt, wriggled across the hard-packed dirt to a spot below the office window where the indirect spillage of light was sufficient to my acclimated eyes to observe the territory I was hired to peruse.

Methodically I scanned the grounds. There was a feeling, a sixth sense, a tightening at the gut level. This was the time something was going to happen.

It occurs to me now, as it did then, that I was a fool to be protecting property without a gun, since I was skinny and had no experience in hand-to-hand. To bust somebody in the chops with my truncheon would necessitate getting closer than I wanted to be. My fingers strayed to the handcuffs on my belt. No problem with what to do—just how to get there.

The fool had shined his shoes. I missed the deduction. In the shadow of the wall across the alley from the open-roofed, half-constructed building with the copper tubing, I saw the trailer light reflected with clarity on the caps of his spit-shined cordovans.

No question about it. He was checking out the light at the guard-post window above my prone body. I could sneak back out the other side of the trailer skirt, swiftly circle the building, and come up behind him. He wasn't moving now, but would he still be there? Right now I was certain of his position. That was an advantage.

A light breeze carried the palpable aroma of skunk. In the distance I heard the bark of a dog. Headlights of a single car with its brights on passed on the parkway beyond the deserted parking lot. I thought for a second that the intruder was wearing a baseball cap. Maybe a windbreaker. The bricks of the building support stood out from the fascia only about four inches. It was enough to conceal but not to hide this figure as patient as I.

He thought, I presumed, that I was goofing off in the trailer. Thus at this moment the advantage was mine, the advantage of the righteous salaried employee over the sneak thief with no healthy reason for being out at night.

He hunkered down into a sprinter's crouch and in the blink of an eye he was across the alley and into the construction zone. Tableaux are made to break. He was on my turf, watching the trailer window from a new vantage point where the shine of his shoes mattered little. Though I could no longer see him, it seemed logical that was what he was doing. Being careful. That was part of his pattern.

My first duty was clear: call the cops. My second duty was in my job description: hold him until the cops arrive. That was for my benefit as well as the agency's. That was so the client knew his money was well spent. The intruder would run from the cops when he heard them coming, saw the lights. He might get away. I might have to reenact this darkling waltz. Next time it might not accommodate my pleasure. This time the advantage was clearly mine. I belly-crawled quickly under the trailer and made my way through the silent magnet-latched aluminum door, through the bathroom light-lock. Sitting on the floor, I dialed the cops.

"This is the security guard at the construction site in Brickville. I have a possible perpetrator. I will apprehend said perpetrator in trespass. Better get here."

Cosh ready in my right hand, I went into the character of the stumblebum guard. I made my exit from the backlighted trailer door, flooding the entrance to the dusty amphitheater with yellow incandescent light. I was the well-rehearsed actor embarking on his greatest entrance.

Only performance can validate planning. My aforementioned hobby of weaponry had taken a rather funky and direct turn.

Dynamite fuse is timed to an inch a second. Dynamite fuse will burn underwater, unlike the fuse of a cherry bomb, the timing of which is unpredictable in the extreme. Never throw a cherry bomb. It might explode in your hand and shred your fingers. Dynamite fuse is predictable. You could, if you wanted, bundle a number of fuses together, as I had done. I relit the Macanudo and started my hastily made timing device with the cigar for a punk.

Silently counting the seconds, I ran toward the empty maw of the pit-black depth of the building. I went in low, rolling to a combat stance behind a pile of loading pallets just as the *whump whump* of my twin tennis ball mortars quivered the ground. A couple of seconds later, white, puffy like flak, the tennis balls exploded at the periphery of my vision, arcing down from their apogee a millisecond late for a perfect shot. I would remember to shorten the fuses next time. Quite pretty, but I hadn't time to savor the pyrotechnics as I was scanning the enclosure for a glimpse of the intruder in the windbreaker.

I glimpsed the prone figure in the brief flaklight just as the lawn-umbrella popcorn shotguns exploded, showering the building's interior with the haillike rattle of ricocheting kernels—harmless but distracting. The intruder's face was buried in the soft dirt. It was short work to bop him on the cap with the weighted end of my cosh and cuff his hands behind him, pulling his shoulder sockets to the point of dislocation and none too gently grinding my knee into the small of his back as the screaming sirens and lights swung into the parking lot and lit the site with flashes that reminded me of a grotesque rock 'n' roll dance hall.

"He's yours, boys," I said to the approaching cops. I let them pull my boss to his feet, to the toes of his spit-shined cordovans, stumbling and incoherent, but not too demoralized to fire me on the spot. The reason my boss had taken back his pistol was that he had decided to sneak up on me to find out if I was doing a proper job.

I was proud of myself, though. I'd nailed him before he had a chance to draw.

Hollywood Detective

RON GOULART

Ron Goulart has had many identities. He was "Avenger" series author Kenneth Robeson; as Con Steffanson he adapted the "Flash Gordon" comic strip and the "Laverne and Shirley" television series into novels; and as Frank Shawn he did the same for the "Phantom" comic strip; as Josephine Kains he has written mysteries; and using house pseudonym Zeke Masters, he has written Westerns. He is best known as a science fiction writer, the heir to Kurt Vonnegut as the genre's leading humorist, in the opinion of New Statesman *reviewer Martin Amis. The unifying element in Ron Goulart's career is that he is a popular-fiction historian, a bent that informs this story.*

A COUPLE OF HIKERS were the first to spot him in the misty morning woods in the canyon above Hollywood. They hurried back, knapsacks rattling, to the nearest highway and managed to flag down two cops in a patrol car.

He was still on the mossy ground when the two uniformed young men got there. He was wearing a heavy New York overcoat that was much too warm for California in early April, his broad back against the trunk of an oak tree and a brand-new shovel resting across his knees.

The officers were named Robinson and Konheim. Robinson was the lean, blond one and he had his revolver out, aimed at the man with the shovel.

Officer Konheim, dark-haired and just an inch over the required height, moved cautiously closer. "Could you perhaps tell us, sir, what the trouble is?"

The man was heavyset, his short-cropped black hair graying. He blinked at the two officers. "I'm suffering from a failure of nerve," he said in a slightly raspy voice. "It all started, so help me, as a literary quest. A pilgrimage, you might say."

Officer Konheim spoke to his partner out of the side of his mouth. "I've seen this guy's picture someplace. In a mug book or—"

"Book jacket." The seated man cleared his throat.

"Sure, that's it." Brightening, Officer Konheim suddenly snapped his fingers.

Officer Robinson flinched. "What did I tell you about all the time doing that while I've got my piece out?"

"You're Fredric Sherwin, aren't you, sir?"

"I thought so, up until yesterday."

"Right. Your newest mystery novel, *Dead Before You Know It,* has been on the best-seller lists for a dozen weeks."

"Twenty-three weeks," corrected Sherwin.

"This guy's some kind of writer?"

"Yeah, he's done five books about a tough Hollywood private eye named Joe Tennyson."

"Seven," said the seated author.

"And he's just about the best-selling mystery writer, except for Mitch Gunnerson."

"That heavy-handed hack has never outsold me." Sherwin used his newly purchased shovel to lean on while he grunted to his feet. "I've got sales figures in one of my pockets to prove beyond a doubt that he—"

"That's right; you were on a talk show the other day, flashing those figures." Officer Konheim, remembering, chuckled. "You called Gunnerson some great names, got off some terrific insults. You said his private-eye novels about Jock Bricker were a lot of crap."

"That doesn't," said Officer Robinson, "sound like such a terrific—"

"He's paraphrasing me," explained the detective novelist, crossing his hands over the handle of the new shovel.

Officer Konheim said, "According to that TV interview, Mr. Sherwin, you came out here from New York to work on a screenplay based on one of your—"

"Based on *Might As Well Die*, yes. Television movie for Hollywood Video Productions," said the writer. "My first trip out here to the Coast, or so I thought."

"Do," asked Konheim, "your reasons for being here in the wilderness have anything to do with the movie?"

Shaking his head, Sherwin answered, "Has more to do with my past."

Officer Robinson said, "A while ago you told us it had something to do with a literary pilgrimage."

"They're all linked, my past and my books. Although I wasn't aware of that until yesterday . . . was it yesterday? Yes . . . I didn't know that when I began my quest. If you fellows have a few minutes, I can explain."

Robinson kicked at the loamy ground. "Has a crime been perpetrated, sir?" Impatience showed in his voice. "Because otherwise—"

"Murder," said Sherwin.

"Murder?" echoed both officers, glancing around.

Easing himself down onto a fallen log and setting the bright shovel aside, the writer said, "It'll take, you know, a few minutes to make it all clear."

After holstering his gun, Robinson took out his pocket notebook. "Guess you'd better tell us exactly what you mean, sir."

Konheim found another log and sat. "Maybe we ought to read you your rights."

"Plenty of time for that," said Sherwin.

The mist was growing thicker, closing in around the three of them.

The Beverly Vista Hotel sits (began Sherwin) like a tired old dowager in the hills above Hollywood, trying desperately to hide its age and wipe away all its forlorn memories of the greats and near-greats who've come to grief in its high-ceilinged suites and corridors. I woke up in my Beverly Vista suite about noon three days

211

ago, feeling like one of those memories the hotel was trying to forget.

My head felt like a recording studio where six or seven rock groups had just finished an all-night session. Worse, I couldn't remember whom I'd been with the night before, nor what had become of her.

That sort of thing, as I'll explain, bothers me. I don't like to forget things, mostly because I've managed to forget completely the first thirty years of my life.

I was untangling myself from sleep and silken sheets when I got a hell of a shock. I thought I was dying and hearing my own death rattle.

But the sound, though it was about as pleasant as the noise your coffin lid'll make shutting on you for the last time, had a chipper note. Besides which, it wasn't emanating from me.

Someone outside my door was producing it. "You better be up and ready in there, Sherwin. Not that I mean to be a nag or disrespectful, because after all, you're writing the *You May As Well Drop Dead* script for HVP and I'm one of their publicity people and so—"

"*Might As Well Die!*" I bellowed, stumbling free of the bed.

"Beg pardon?" The thumping she'd been producing as an accompaniment to her caterwauling, a pounding that was as disheartening as that of the hoofbeats of the Four Horsemen of the Apocalypse, with Roy Rogers bringing up the rear, ceased.

"C'mon in, Riorita."

The door opened and a slim, pretty blond young woman eased in. She was wearing white designer jeans, a blazer that had apparently previously belonged to a circus giant, and no bra. "Far be it from me, Sherwin, to criticize," she said, "but you look like somebody they just pulled out of an earthquake in South America. We have to be over at KBZ-TV in exactly . . ." Sliding up the enormous sleeve of her coat, she consulted her digital watch. ". . . Holy Toledo. We're six hours late. . . . Oh, no, that's right. I have my watch set to Nova Scotia time."

"Riorita, I'm not even going to ask you why." Tottering, I made my way into the immense white-and-gold bath chamber.

"Actually," said Riorita McAllister, "we have forty-six minutes to get there. Yes, I think if I drive at a reckless and foolhardy pace along the freeway, I can deliver you to 'Lunch with Mr. and Mrs. Belch' in time for—"

"Ugh."

"What's that?"

"Nothing, Riorita." I'd made the mistake of viewing myself in the vast mirror over the sink. I resembled something that had just surfaced in the Black Lagoon.

"This is cute," she said out in the bedroom as I commenced shaving.

"What?"

"The way you have all the favorable reviews of *Dead Before You Know It* taped around the walls. Some good usable quotes here . . . I wonder if this kind of tape'll take the flock off the wallpaper, though. Well,

213

hell, considering what we're paying per day for this setup, I guess we're entitled to a little flock . . . oh no. Oh, I hope you aren't going to mention this on the interview today, the way you went and did yesterday."

"I will," I called above the deadly hum of the electric razor, knowing what she was alluding to.

"But the purpose of all these damn interviews is to alert people about *You Just As Well Better Be Dead.* So that when it airs this fall, and we fly you out here again for more PR, everybody'll be worked up to a fever pitch. They'll be dying to see Joe Tennyson come to life on their television screens and—"

"The paperback private-eye novels written by Frank Sultan, whoever he was, in the late 1950s and early 1960s were a great source of comfort and inspiration to me. When I lost my memory, they—"

"That's another thing." She was framed in the doorway, eyeing me. "Downplay the amnesia stuff. It makes some people uneasy, wondering if you're goofy or—"

"Amnesia's a staple of television drama, so—"

"But in real life, I mean, it causes viewers to suspect that maybe you're . . . can you suck in your stomach any?"

"If offered sufficient incentives."

"Well, we don't want you looking too flabby. Course, you'll be sitting behind the lunch table, so most of that won't show."

"Good, I won't even have to zip my fly."

"That's the kind of quip you have to watch, too," Riorita said, giving me a bleak smile and reminding

214

me of a skeleton I'd met once in a catacomb down in Mexico. "Oh, and don't hit too hard on your feud with Mitch Gunnerson. Maybe you just ought not to mention him or his books at all. What I mean is, originally we were going to adapt one of his novels and then decided to do you instead."

"I know that, child. It was I, working through my gang of insidious and heartless agents, who convinced Hollywood Video Productions to dump that stooge and—"

"That's why you should behave like a good sport, Sherwin. Crowing over your defeated opponent isn't cricket."

"G'wan, people love that. Don't you watch wrestling?"

"No, mostly I watch PBS."

"I was alluding to 'Masterpiece Wrestling.'"

Her nose wrinkled. "Get out of those strange PJs and into some clothes. We have to rush. . . . Oh, and don't put on anything that's as New York as that suit you wore yesterday."

Bill and Betty Belch were beautiful people, in their middle thirties. The sort of perfect couple you find only in southern California or atop a wedding cake. Their talk show was broadcast from a set that looked like a patio dining area. The artificial sunlight, however, didn't have sufficient eye-scorching glare, and there wasn't that acrid smell of exhaust fumes and compromised dreams in the air.

215

Both the Belches smiled at me nonstop, with those rigid grimaces you see on show-business types and dead cats.

Midway through the same old interview I got to feeling like one of Pavlov's dogs. I reached into the pocket of my tweedy sport coat, therefore, and produced a copy of *Casket for a Blonde,* by Frank Sultan.

Off camera, Riorita began wrinkling her nose and making negative hand signals and muttering in an unhappy silent language.

I ignored her. "Betty, I'll tell you another reason for my first trip to Los Angeles," I said into the camera. "Years ago, the detective novels of a marvelous writer who called himself Frank Sultan got me through a very rough period. I'm certain he lived out here, and I'm hoping to be able to locate him and have a visit."

Bill Belch said, "We've heard something about your interest in Frank Sultan before, haven't we, Betty?"

"We surely have, Bill. How Fred Sherwin's been trying to track down the writer behind the Sultan pen name for years, to thank him for those private-eye novels he wrote years ago. Six of them, wasn't it, Fred?"

"Five. *Casket for a Blonde* was the first novel to feature Harry Dream, Hollywood Detective. That came out as a Class Paperback in 1959. The final novel, *Slab for a Redhead,* was published in 1965. Class Books, by the way, was a moderate-sized firm based in Los Angeles."

"But long out of business, isn't that right?"

"Yes, Bill." I held up the book and tapped its cover.

216

"Haven't had much luck tracking down the company from a distance, but I'm hoping I can do better on the spot."

Betty Belch said, with a touch of sadness in her smiling voice, "I think our many viewers would like to know why these particular books are so important to our guest, Fredric Sherwin, don't you, Bill?"

"I do, yes, Betty. Do you mind talking about your . . . um . . . amnesia, Fred?"

"Not at all. I'm not ashamed of it." I set the Harry Dream novel down beside my plate.

Crouched low, Riorita was gesturing wildly at me from behind one of the cameras. The big sleeves on her blazer flapped like the arms of a windmill as she mouthed, "Plug the movie! Plug the damn movie!"

Instead I told Bill and Betty Belch and their millions of viewers about my life. How I'd awakened in a freight yard in New Haven, Connecticut, some twenty years ago. I appeared to be in my early thirties and had absolutely no recollection of who I was. Quite recently I'd been hit on the head with something hard and probably metallic, but I didn't remember that either. There wasn't a speck of identification on me.

While I was recovering in a charity ward, the local police tried to find out who I really was. They never succeeded. I had never, so they concluded, been in the armed forces, never had a driver's license, so far as they could tell. My fingerprints weren't on file anywhere. My description matched that of several missing persons, including an embezzler from Baton Rouge

217

and a stockbroker who'd gone out for a beer in Iola, Wisconsin, a year before and never come home. Turned out I wasn't any of them.

In the hospital I read the paperback novel I'd found in my coat pocket. It was *Casket for a Blonde.* Sultan was a first-rate writer, as good as Raymond Chandler and better than any of the apes who tried to imitate Chandler. He had a fresh, original voice and he wrote about the Los Angeles area like nobody else. I was hooked and I got a nurse to buy the rest of the Harry Dream, Hollywood Detective, novels at a secondhand book shop. You could still find them back then.

Those novels had a profound effect on me. Although I never have been able to find out who I was during the first three decades of my life nor what I'd done to earn a living, Frank Sultan's novels gave me the profession I've followed since I was reborn in New Haven two decades ago.

Once I became successful, I tried to track down Frank Sultan. We all of us, at one time or another, have an urge to communicate with an author, an actor, someone whose work has touched us deeply and profoundly. I owe a lot to Frank Sultan, but I've never been able to find out anything about him. He never wrote another book, under that name or any other, I'm sure, from 1965 to this day. Class Books, who were located in Santa Monica, went bankrupt in 1967. All their records seem to have been destroyed. I've written letters to mystery fanzines, bookshops, special collection libraries, in hope—

———

218

"Sir," cut in Officer Robinson, hunching his back and flexing his fingers, "you aren't anywhere near to explaining why we've found you sitting in among the oaks with a shovel in your lap."

"I came to do some digging, but I haven't been able to work up the nerve," said Sherwin. "What I'm trying to do is give you a report of the facts. The way Joe Tennyson does, the way Harry Dream—"

"Yeah, but that usually takes a whole book. We don't—"

"Let Mr. Sherwin explain it his own way." Officer Konheim had his elbows resting on his knees and was leaning toward the seated author. "I saw you on that lunch show you've been talking about, sir. That's where you read some stuff out of a Harry Dream novel and then out of a recent PI novel by Mitch Gunnerson."

"Betty Belch . . . or mayhap it was Bill Belch . . . one of the set anyway. It was suggested that Gunnerson was also a follower of the Chandler-Sultan school," Sherwin said, coughing into the thickening fog. "I simply read comparable passages and showed that comparing Gunnerson to Sultan was like comparing elephant droppings to chocolate mousse. You may've noticed an off-camera groan while I was doing that. Riorita McAllister."

"About your being here," persisted Robinson. "And what about a murder?"

"We would," added Konheim, "like to hear about that eventually, sir."

219

The day was dying and I felt like I was going with it. Sprawled on the bed in my suite, nursing a glass of white wine, I had the momentary impression that the entire room was lined with white satin. Just like the inside of a coffin.

When the phone tolled I let it go for ten or so rings before, reluctantly, I picked it up. "Yeah?"

"Would this perhaps be Fredric Sherwin?"

"It would."

"Ah."

"How about telling me who you are."

He had a voice like a man who'd just gargled with gasoline. "Perhaps my name means nothing to you. I'm Daredevil Dumphrey."

His name meant nothing to me. "And so?"

"You may have heard of my little bookshop here in Oil Beach."

"A mystery bookshop?" I thought I'd checked out just about every one of those in the country in my quest for information about Frank Sultan, but I didn't recall one in that town.

"You've hit it squarely. I operate the Crime Does Pay Bookshop. The name is a play on the famous—"

"Yeah, I guessed that almost at once," I told him. "Let me explain, Mr. Dumphrey, that I don't have any first editions of my books to sell you, that I don't have the time to come to Oil Beach for an autographing session so you can boost the price of every one of my—"

"I can help you find Frank Sultan."

"Huh?"

"You mentioned on the TV earlier in the day that you'd be interested in finding him. Took me this long to find out where you were residing during your stay. I really had to act like Joe Tennyson in order to track—"

"You know where Sultan is?"

"Let us say rather that I know someone who might. Would it be in order for me to ask if some sort of honorarium is involved?"

"Fifty bucks."

"A hundred would be more satisfying."

"You got it," I said. "Are you at the shop? I can drive my rented car down to—"

"Ah. Due to a recent fire, the shop is padlocked. I can be found, however, at a seaside bistro named Hardtack Nancy's every evening. Can you drop in at eight tonight?"

"Sure. How sure are you that—"

"Eight, then." He hung up.

It wasn't until sundown yesterday that I reached Exene Patton. Before finding her I had to talk with Daredevil Dumphrey and then follow the labyrinthine trail he directed me to. After I met him at Hardtack Nancy's bar, a forlorn bistro that smelled of moldering sawdust, spilled beer, and lost innocence, he told me that a year or so ago he'd had an encounter with an elderly woman who'd come into his bookshop to sell a carton of old mystery paperbacks. When Dumphrey saw that they were all fine-condition copies of very rare Class Books —including all five of Frank Sultan's Harry Dream,

Hollywood Detective, novels—he got so excited he actually payed her nearly.25 percent of what the books were worth. It turned out she was the widow of Norm Klassenberg, the long-deceased publisher of the Class line.

Dumphrey hadn't asked her about the identity of Frank Sultan, but he was certain the old woman knew and would be able to tell me. All I had to do was slip him the agreed-upon hundred and he'd provide the address. His nickname of Daredevil, by the way, he'd picked up in the days when he worked as a Hollywood stuntman. "I probably worked in most of the B-movies and serials that thrilled you in your childhood," he told me after his second draft beer. I told him that might well be, but I had no recollection of what had or hadn't thrilled me in my youth.

The Widow Klassenberg had no telephone. When I reached the decaying stucco apartment house that was perched like an undecided suicide on a forlorn bluff overlooking the black Pacific, I was informed by the manager that she had died three months ago.

He was a small man, exactly one inch too tall to be classed a midget, he informed me, and he suggested I might want to look through the steamer trunk she'd left in the basement. The fee for that was fifty dollars. I tried to talk him down to twenty-five, the way Joe Tennyson does with informers in my novels, but that only made him threaten to hike the price to one hundred.

The basement was as chill and damp as Mrs.

Klassenberg's grave, and I expected to have the old lady herself sit up and glare at me when I lifted the lid of the battered trunk.

Inside I beheld a jumble of ancient clothes, smelling of mothballs and sadness, nearly fifty copies of various Class titles, and then a bundle of letters. Reading the letters took quite some time. The light from the single 40-watt bulb overhead wasn't sufficient for easy reading, and the manager kept tromping down every few minutes to interrupt me with intimate anecdotes about his misspent, but basically dull, life. "Do you know what it feels like to be rejected by a freak show because you're too tall?" he'd inquire. "Have you ever been turned down for a date by a lady who was just five-foot-one on the grounds you was too petite?"

Eventually I got through all the letters, some of which dated back to 1949. They weren't business letters, mostly being from friends and relatives. There were three recent ones from an Exene Patton. In the most recent she said, "Strangely enough, I still miss those days when I was assistant bookkeeper for you and Norm at Class." A bookkeeper paid the bills, wrote the checks for the authors. She'd know who Frank Sultan really was.

Once Exene Patton had been a very pretty woman; there were still clues to that in what was left of her. She was a few years younger than I am, in her late forties someplace. Thin and gaunt, her hair a tangled gray. The hazy twilight seeping into the narrow living room of her faded apartment in Santa Monica didn't hide the ruin of her face.

Setting aside her tumbler of scotch, she reached out a thin arm to turn on the floor lamp. She was sprawled in a bloated sofa chair, wearing a terry-cloth bathrobe that was from another decade of her life. "You still don't remember me, do you, Frank?"

From the lamé straight-back chair facing her I said, "You've got it wrong, Mrs. Patton. My name is Fredric Sherwin."

"Now, yes."

Frowning, I said, "As I tried to explain to you on the phone, I'm looking for Frank Sultan."

She started to laugh and it was awful. The laughter took over her nearly fleshless body, shaking it. She coughed, nearly choked. Her skin faded to a gray that was the color of funeral ashes.

I started to move to help her, but she waved me back with one gaunt hand.

After a moment she took a gulp of her drink, coughed a few more times, and then lit a fresh cigarette from the stub of the old one. "Good thing I don't laugh much these days, isn't it, Frank?"

"You're still getting me mixed up with—"

"Hey, you really aren't kidding." She was staring at me, a little color sneaking back into her face. "You don't remember me at all."

"Far as I know we've never—"

"I've read a little about you, but I wasn't sure if—"

"You're hinting that I knew you before?"

"Frank, we were lovers."

224

My chair legs scraped the floor as I pushed back in it. "Oh, so? Where was that?"

"Here." A smile touched her sunken face. "Not in this hole. Here in LA, I mean. Twenty years ago. I really, for a long time, thought you must be dead and gone. By the time I noticed your picture on a book jacket . . . only a year or so ago . . . hell, by then it was too late to bother."

"I have no recollection of—"

"Yeah, I was afraid his hitting you on the head like that might've—"

"Who hit me?"

"My husband." She watched me for a few seconds, eyes narrowed. "You don't remember him either . . . Ed Zultanofsky? The two of you, Frank Sherwood and—"

"That was my name?" I rubbed my fingers across my forehead. "That must be why I christened myself Fredric Sherwin . . . I remembered a little."

Exene coughed. "You and Ed teamed up to write for Class Books. I had the job of accountant with old Klassenberg and he was . . . well, fond of me. I helped set up the deal. You guys took your first name and a modified version of Ed's last name to become—"

"Frank Sultan." The sudden realization made me stand up. "All these long years I've been hunting for myself."

"And for Ed," she added. "Although that part's impossible."

"Meaning what?"

"He's dead and buried."

225

"When did that—"

"The night you disappeared," she told me. "That was the same night you killed him."

The fog had closed in even further. Sherwin turned up the collar of his overcoat, thrust both hands deep into his pockets. "As it was explained to me, Ed Zultanofsky had trailed me to one of our rendezvous spots. A cottage a few miles from here. We fought and I knocked him out. I don't remember any of this, but Exene says I persuaded her we had to get rid of him. Bury him here in the woods and make it look as though he'd run out on her. Apparently he was something of a drunk and given to wandering off for days at a time."

Officer Konheim asked, "How did you and this Zultanofsky write the books . . . who did what?"

"Hm?" Sherwin glanced across at him. "I never thought to ask. My guess'd be that he plotted them and I did the actual writing. Since—"

"What about your amnesia?" cut in Officer Robinson. "How'd the woman explain that?"

"Ed apparently came to just after we got him here," answered the writer. "There was another fight and he managed to whack me several times in the head with the spade we'd bought to bury him with. Then, according to Exene, I shot him. We had brought the gun along to use on him. I passed out after that. She dragged his body off into the woods and buried it." He pointed off to his left. "When she came back to where she'd left me, I was gone."

"What happened to you?"

226

"It's her notion that I must've made my way down to the highway," answered Sherwin. "Whoever picked me up rolled me, dumped me in a freight car, and I guess some hobo must have taken pity on me." He tugged a cocktail napkin out of his overcoat pocket. "She drew me a map of where Ed Zultanofsky is buried. After I left her place, I bought a shovel and headed here. But I lost my nerve before I got to the grave and I decided just to sit down for a while."

Robinson shook his head. "Farfetched."

Konheim frowned at his partner. "What do you mean? It sounds—"

"Sounds like a paperback detective plot," Robinson said. "You know what I think, Mr. Sherwin?"

Slowly, wheezing some, Sherwin got up. "Afraid not, Officer."

"You've been bad-mouthing this rival of yours . . . Mitch Gunnerson, isn't it?" Robinson waited until Sherwin had given an affirmative nod. "I think he caught you on that talk show and decided to play a joke on you. A hoax rigged up to scare you and make a fool of you."

"That possibility hadn't occurred to me."

Officer Konheim looked from the writer to his partner. "Me either."

"Well," said Robinson, picking up the new shovel and handing it to Sherwin, "let's go and find out for sure."

Subscription to THE NEW BLACK MASK
$27.80/year in the U.S.

Subscription correspondence should be sent to
THE NEW BLACK MASK
129 West 56th Street
New York, NY 10019